Dear Reader,
Open the doors of your heart and
let the Sunrays illumine it!

"Test all your actions, words, thoughts on this touchstone: Will this be approved by God? Will this rebound to His renown?"

— BABA

A collection of Inspirational Short Stories, presented with devotion and love at the lotus feet of our beloved Lord Bhagwan Sri Sathya Sai Baba.

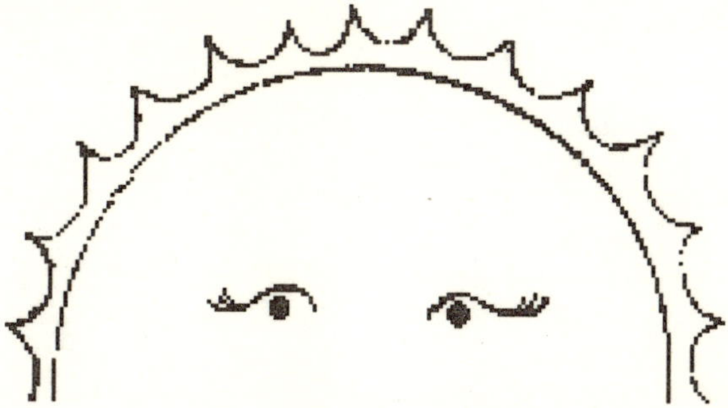

Sunrays for Saturday

(A collection of Inspirational Short stories)

Priya and Sanjay Tandon

PRABHAT
PRAKASHAN

Published by
PRABHAT PRAKASHAN PVT. LTD.
4/19 Asaf Ali Road,
New Delhi-110 002 (INDIA)
e-mail: prabhatbooks@gmail.com

ISBN 978-93-5266-990-5
SUNRAYS FOR SATURDAY
by Priya and Sanjay Tandon
Sketches, Art work and Painting on the cover *by* Priya S. Tandon

Edition
First, 2018
Second, 2021
Third, 2025

Paperback Price
₹ 500.00 (Rupees Five Hundred only)

Printed at
R-Tech Offset Printers, Delhi

Sanjay Tandon with Bhagwan Sri Sathya Sai Baba

Priya S. Tandon with Bhagwan Sri Sathya Sai Baba

Dedication

Dedicated to our Beloved Lord Bhagwan Baba,
Who is not only our sole mate,
but also our soul mate;
Who is not only our sole refuge,
but also our soul's refuge!

Priya and Sanjay Tandon

The manuscript of this book was offered for blessings at the Mahasamadhi of our beloved Lord Bhagwan Sri Sathya Sai Baba on the holy day of Guru Poornima, July 27, 2018 at Prashanti Nilayam, Puttaparthi, Andhra Pradesh, India.

Prayer

Dear Lord,

As the Sunrays come round full circle,
It is an emotional moment, a miracle!

As this blessed script nears completion,
Our hearts pound as if in rendition!

Pray keep us attuned, engaged in your work,
For life would be barren without this perk!

The making of this book brings bliss to us,
Let it spread love and peace beyond us!

It is in consummation the candle passes the test,
For your mission Oh Sai! We are at your behest!

— Priya and Sanjay Tandon

पीयूष गोयल
Piyush Goyal

रेल एवं कोयला मंत्री
भारत सरकार
Minister of Railways and coal
Government of India

Foreword

Books are windows that open a whole new world for all of us. They are also beacons that influence us in everyday life. The book 'Sunrays for Saturday', is a compilation of 52 short stories that carry a message for all of us. The authors Priya & Sanjay Tandon, like expert jewellers, have picked 52 gems from varied sources including our rich heritage. Each story is inspirational and appeals to all walks of life whether they be old or young, a busy working professional or those who stay at home.

This book is part of a unique series that started with 'Sunrays for Sundays', and will encourage people to read at least once a week for a whole year. The simple style and engrossing stories make it an effortless read. I would advise readers to keep the entire collection of seven books and read one story each day of the week. I bet most will finish the stories long before the 52 weeks are over.

Piyush Goyal

Rail Bhawan, new Delhi-110001, Tel. : +91-1123386645, 23381213 Fax : +91-11-23387333
e-mail. : piyush.goyal@gov.in, Website : www.piyushgoyal.in

Politics without principles,
Education without character,
Science without humanity, and
Commerce without morality
Are not only useless, but
positively dangerous.

—Sathya Sai Baba

Foreword

17th July, 2018

It is really heartening to see Priya and Sanjay put their thoughts together to write an inspiring and thought-provoking book to help guide thousands of readers. I absolutely admire their efforts and the motivation they provide in this valuable compendium.

With the seventh book in the Sunrays series - the Sunrays for Saturdays - they have captured the essence of the smaller yet very important things in our lives and have woven beautiful stories around them. We might fail to notice such things in our busy lives, but they are extremely important.

Priya and Sanjay have found an invaluable medium to convey their values, their ideas and more importantly their voice to the people from all walks of life in a powerful-yet-subtle way. They have indeed taken up a noble cause of spreading positivity and thereby touching lives of many. I wish them all the very best for not just Sunrays for Saturdays, but many more such endeavours in the times to come.

Vijay Shekhar Sharma
Founder & CEO-Paytm

One97 Communications Limited, B-121, Sector-5, Noida-201301, India
Regd Office : 1st Floor, Devika Tower, Nehru Place, New Delhi-110019, India
CIN: U72200DL2000PLC108985
T: +91 120 4770770, F: +91 120 4770771, billing@one97.com, www.One97.com

If you honour your mother,
the Mother of the universe
will guard you against harm.
If you honour your father,
the Father of all Beings will guard you.
If you honour your parents,
your children will honour you.

—Sathya Sai Baba

make my trip

Dil toh roaming hai

Foreword

Storytelling is an important part of all cultures and as the digital age brings down human attention span, there can't be a better way to share wisdom, warmth and compassion than through short stories. By penning Sunrays Series Priya and Sanjay have compiled beautiful anecdotes and inspirational thoughts that warms the hearts while imparting values and wisdom.

Sunrays for Saturday is the seventh book of this series and like all the previous ones it's a profound collection of stories that will purposefully resonate with the readers. These stories are meant for everybody and will appeal to all age groups and people from all professions as it provides food for thought to all.

I am sure you will enjoy reading this book and find it as uplifting as I did. My best wishes for the success of this book to Priya and Sanjay Tandon.

Deep Kalra
Founder & Group CEO

MakeMyTrip (India) Pvt. Ltd.: 19th Floor-Tower B, Building No. 5, (Epitome), DLF Cyber City, DLF Phase III, Gurgaon -122002 Haryana
Tel: +91 124 439 5000 Fax: +91 124 439 5100
Regd. Office : UG -07, (Front Side) TDI Mall Rajouri Garden, New Delhi- 27,
Tel: +91 11 4352 8687, Fax: +91 11 4352 8688
CIN :U63040DL2000PTC105210 I website: www.makemytrip.com

If there is righteousness in the heart,
There will be beauty in character.
If there is beauty in character,
There will be harmony in the home.
When there is harmony in the home,
There will be order in the nation.
When there is order in the nation,
There will be peace in the world.
So, be righteous; avoid all
prejudices against others on the
basis of caste, creed, colour, mode of
worship, status or degree of affluence.
Do not look down on any one;
look upon all as Divine as you really are.

—Sathya Sai Baba

Preface

The Sunrays books are purely a composite reverberation of the convergence of the synergies of love, inspiration and devotion. In putting together these books, we have felt blissfully connected to Bhagwan Baba and had the opportunity to understand the beauty of His teachings.

All our books have a picture of the Sun on their cover page. Their covers have had bands of the rainbow colours of violet, blue, green, yellow, orange and red. Now the seventh book has been released with an indigo colour band. This is the last of the Sunrays series. The seven colours of the Rainbow, i.e., the VIBGYOR being completed, it feels like we have succeeded in painting a rainbow across the sky. The Rainbow or *Indradhanush* is a seven-coloured semi-circular formation across the sky. On extremely rare occasions, there is a complete circular formation in the sky with seven colours. This is called *Brahma Dhanush*.

According to Wikipedia, "...a rainbow is, in fact, a full circle, we usually only see the half arc of it due to our positioning in respect to it; if you were to be positioned higher up (such as on a tall building or an airplane), then you could view its actual full circle..."

As I write this, a thought comes to my mind... with the release of this book; the half arc of the rainbow has been completed by us. The other half which is not visible is within us; it is within you and me. When we as humans blossom with good character, when we become good human beings, when we succeed in exuding the love within, to all those we come into contact with, when we become truly Baba's *Premaswaroopularaas* (embodiments of love); it is then that the other half of the rainbow will be visible!

Dear Readers, when we get letters from people of different communities the world over, telling us how they are using these books, to help themselves or others become better, we feel that the Rainbow is coming around full circle. It is no longer just an *Indra Dhanush*, it is becoming a *Brahma Dhanush!*

I usually take a quick look at my e-mail on the phone in the morning. I look up first of all, the 'Sai Inspires from Prashanti Nilayam' sent by the Radio Sai Team in the morning. The format of that email is such that on one side is a picture of Bhagwan Baba, and next to it is an excerpt from one of His discourses. With my hypermetropia-afflicted eyes, I am unable to read small print now. So, first of all, I enjoy His picture; then I zoom into the text and enlarge it on my touchscreen phone, such that Swami's picture moves out of the frame and I am able to read the text easily. Up until some months back, doing this would make me feel terrible, that I push the Lord's form out of the way to read some content. But now I am at peace with it because Swami told me that His picture (physical form) was there in the beginning only to attract. Later, we have to let go of the physical form and concentrate only on His teachings.

He took away the physical form that we loved so dearly, so that we could concentrate on what He had come to give us. Reminiscing, I smile as I recollect Him saying that He gives us all that we ask for in the hope that someday we would ask for that which He had really come to give. His teachings are the real treasure... and it is now that we realise it! What we need to do is to transform His physical absence into His spiritual presence.

Come to think of it, all the pictures we have today of Lord Rama or Krishna who walked the Earth aeons ago are made the way they have been imagined by artists. There were no photographs in those times. But the teachings and stories of their lives are documented in the scriptures and, more importantly, are passed on from generation to generation as part of our scriptures, culture and folklore.

Baba donned the physical form so that He could walk with us, talk to us, love us and teach us to love Him. But that beloved physical form too had an expiry date. The Lord too conformed to the Laws of birth and death that He laid down for us all. So, the sooner we detach ourselves from His physicality, the better it is for us. Much as we loved dearly, Swami's petite physical form, we are slowly learning to connect with 'Him' in the form that is resident in us. And then don't we have to live up to the endearment He so often used for us, *'Divyaatma swaroopas!'* (Embodiments of Divinity) We are all trying to achieve the inward concentration and realise the truth that we are *Divya-atmas* (Divine souls) and so we are a part of the *Param-atma*... we are all a part of the whole. I hope one day we shall all realise this and revel in the bliss of realisation.

In the *Kali Yuga*, the path prescribed is of *Namasmarana* (Chanting the name of the Lord). Plant the seedling of devotion, namely the preliminary exercise of remembering the Lord's name *(namasmarana)* in the mind. That will soon grow into a tree with the branches of virtue, service, sacrifice, love, equanimity, fortitude and courage. Swami tells us that we consume food, but are not aware how that food is transformed into energy, intelligence, emotion and health. In the same way, we should just swallow this food for the spirit, this remembrance of the Lord's name, and watch how it gets transmuted into virtue and all things Divine, without our being aware of it.

Devotion is a way of life. It is like an ongoing *Yagna*. The offering which we must make in the *Yagna* is that of our bad thoughts, desires and actions. Devotion has to be full-time if we want full-time grace. Swami says that full-time devotion is very simple. Maintaining equanimity under all circumstances and all the time is full-time devotion.

In today's times, we spend a lot of time on social media. Because strangely we are so concerned about what people think of us. Do we ever pause to reflect upon what God thinks about us?

Really speaking, it doesn't matter whether you are on Linked In ... what matters is, are you really Linked-in? It doesn't matter whether you are able to surf the internet, are you able to surf the Inner net? It doesn't matter if you are on Facebook, can you face the book that holds the record of your thoughts, words and deeds? So let's be conscious of what we are doing. Let us live in the complete awareness of the Lord. Being conscious of the conscience is consciousness! Let us test each action on this touchstone – Will this rebound to His renown?

Let me share that I always offer the first fruit of the season from the Chikoo tree in our home to Baba. This time as I offered it to Him saying, "Swami this is the fruit from our garden…" He replied, "And you are the fruit of my garden!" Oh! I was totally overwhelmed with the thought. Then this thought came bouncing back to me; if I am the fruit of His garden, then I have to be the best… once again… Will I rebound to His renown? I have to do my best to make Him proud!

On a personal front, Swami has been present in our lives both in latent as well as patent form. Our second son, Shiven always said that he would only get married to a girl who is a Sai devotee, for only then would she be able to understand the place Swami had in his life. He recently got married to Sai Vangmayee, a girl from a family of Sai devotees. Our boys Saraansh, Shiven and Satyam have always shared our zeal for the Sunrays project and it is a joy that our two daughters-in-love, Umang and Sai Vangmayee too have joined in the passion. Umang always manages the sale of books whenever we put up a stall and Vangmayee says that she grew up reading the Sunrays books!

I (Priya) recently started writing in the public space. I have a Blog that Swami directed me to name, 'The Cosmic Word'. It can be viewed at this link: http://priya.tandonindia.com/.

Through my Blog and newspaper articles, I feel I get the opportunity to share my thoughts and Swami's teachings in a form and format that is palatable to the common man. This is my humble way of spreading His message. And then I think, "Had I not asked Swami to make me His instrument?" I feel this is the way He has chosen for me to deliver His message. For that, I feel extremely blessed as well as motivated.

And now that the Sunrays have come full circle, perhaps this is the way forward, to keep the cerebral juices flowing and the ink in my pen from drying up.

Dear readers, we sincerely hope you enjoy reading this book as much as or even more than: we as a couple have enjoyed making it.

Each story in the book is based on the teachings of Bhagwan Baba. It is preceded by a quote selected from His myriad discourses and is a humble offering to articulate and explicate it. Besides, it is also illustrated by a simple pencil sketch, so as to leave a lasting impression on the mind of the reader.

May our beloved Bhagwan continue to keep us safe and blessed for ever and ever... Bowing with prayerful salutations at the lotus feet of our most beloved Swami!

— Priya and Sanjay Tandon

Going Digital with Sunrays 2.0

Sunrays continues to be the moral safety net for society through its digital presence. Some of the channels where the inspiration is spread are mentioned below:

Daily Good Thought on Email	**Weekly Blog by Sunrays**
An online email subscription where we send daily mailers with a one liner good thought to thousands of people.	The Sunrays website hosts a thought provoking blog on the intersection of spirituality and modern societal/cultural commentary which gets you thinking.
URL:https://sunraysme.substack.com/subscribe OR Scan:	URL: https://www.sunrays.me/ OR Scan:

Also, the website continues to host the compendium of Weekly Stories published and shared till date since the inception in 2002.

Weekly Sunrays Video on Social: The Sunrays authors went live on social media during the Covid19 lockdown for the first time and haven't looked back since. Every Sunday, you get to hear a new story told with vigour by the duo in Hindi with a brief yet powerful message in the end. The stories are published across all popular social media platforms.

https://www.youtube.com/@SunraysMe or Scan	https://www.instagram.com/sunraysme/ or Scan	https://www.facebook.com/SunraysMe/ or Scan	https://whatsapp.com/channel/0029Vaj KKLSEKyZIG20kTY12 or Scan

Acknowledgements

Howsoever much, we may thank the Lord, it shall never be enough for all that He has blessed us with. When our hearts are inundated with divine thoughts sent by Him, all things worldly just lose their lustre. But, life has to go on till the breath is there in the body. And surely the purpose of life is to live a life with a purpose. We pray that we can live our lives such that our inner purpose is in sync with our outer purpose.

In the making of this book, we have to thank —

The Sri Sathya Sai Sadhna Trust	For accepting these books as donation in kind, and displaying them for sale at the book trust
Mr. Anchal Singh Jamwal	For his devotion and dedication in typing out the handwritten material given to him
Our Parents — Late Smt. Brijpal Tandon and Late Sh. Balramji Dass Tandon (Former Governor of Chattisgarh) Late Mrs. Meera Punchhi and Late Justice Madan Mohan Punchhi (Former Chief Justice of India)	For leading by example and for always encouraging us in this venture
Our Children — Saraansh and his wife Umang Shiven and his wife Sai Vangmayee Satyam and his wife Mahima	For being our strength as well as our weakness; and for always being a huge support in the project
Our Family and Friends	For always being encouraging and so enthusiastic in spreading the good word
Prabhat Prakashan	For publishing the book

All our readers

For so much love!!! We can't thank you enough for the feedback, the love and the accolades!

Thank you Swami for making us walk together in the journey of life. As we strive to make our lives, your message and our hearts overflow with your love, we shall do our best to lead exemplary lives of simplicity, sincerity and discipline. We strive to become rays of sunshine to spread the light and the love and eventually do you proud!

— Priya and Sanjay Tandon

Contents

1

A Date With God

"Some materialists argue that a bird in hand is worth two in the bush. They say that the pleasure you have now should not be given up in the hope of something promised, if and when the pleasure you have is given up. But the happiness of renunciation can be enjoyed here and now, and is much more sustaining and inspiring than the happiness derived from grabbing and attachment."

The well-being of his people was all a king thought about and strove for. Work is worship and Duty is God; so it's no mean conclusion that God was immensely pleased with him. When he was deeply engrossed in prayer, the Lord incarnated and blessed the King. The Lord smiled and told him to ask for anything. The king said, "Oh Lord! You have given me everything. And now after receiving this divine vision, I have nothing left to ask for. But I love my people more than anything. Please grant your vision to them all too!"

God smiled saying that would not be possible. But the king persisted. God said, "Alright, bring your people tomorrow evening to the mountain top and I shall grant them my vision from behind the mountain."

So, the following day the king announced to all his subjects that he would be taking them to see God! They had a date with God! The air was brimming with excitement and fervour. Virtually the entire kingdom was marching towards the mountain, each trying to outdo the others in speed and style. Some carried flowers; others carried gifts and sweets.

As they reached the base of the mountain, they saw a tree on which grew copper coins and leaves. Some of the people leapt that way to gather the coins. The king warned them saying that no one should get distracted by these attractions because today they were going to see God! Despite that, some people gathered up the coins and ran back home.

The rest of them marched up. Sometime later they spotted a tree with silver coins. A number of people plucked the coins off the tree. The more they plucked, the more they grew. The king again warned his people, not to give in to temptation. His warning fell on deaf ears. Those who gathered up the silver coins rushed back home thinking that such opportunities do not come everyday. Meeting God was something they could do another time. And God was always there whenever they would call. Where would He go anyways?

As most of you would have guessed, as they moved further up, they came across a tree laden with gold leaves and coins. Now this one was too hard to resist. People laughed in glee as they filled their pockets with Gold. They even tied the coins into packets using their garments. The king beseeched them to join him so that they could move on to meet God. But the people thought that God could wait for another day in life, but this opportunity wouldn't come again.

All except the king and the queen were smitten by gold. The king had tears in his eyes as the queen held his arm and both continued their journey up.

The peak of the mountain drew closer. Just then they saw a tree laden with diamonds. Oh! The queen took one look at it and with a whoop of joy, started gathering up the glittering stones in her garments. The king begged her to stop. With their weight, some of her garments tore and her naked body was bared to view. The king hung his head in shame. A feeling of disgust and despair overcame him as he realised that he could not influence his wife too to have that burning penchant for God. He could not awaken in her the yearning to give up the worldly attractions so that she could see God.

Eventually the king walked up to the summit of the mountain and sure enough, God was standing there waiting for him. The king joined his hands and started to explain, but God said, "It is okay my child. I knew you would come alone!"

2

A Pinch of Ash

"Many millionaires today are engaged in filling their own belly. They are not prepared to give even a morsel of food as alms to a beggar who stands at their doorstep. What is the use of having such rich men in our country? They are rich only for name's sake, but, in reality, they are the poorest of the poor. Pursue the path of charity and righteousness. Consider others as your own brothers and sisters. Rather, consider them as thyself."

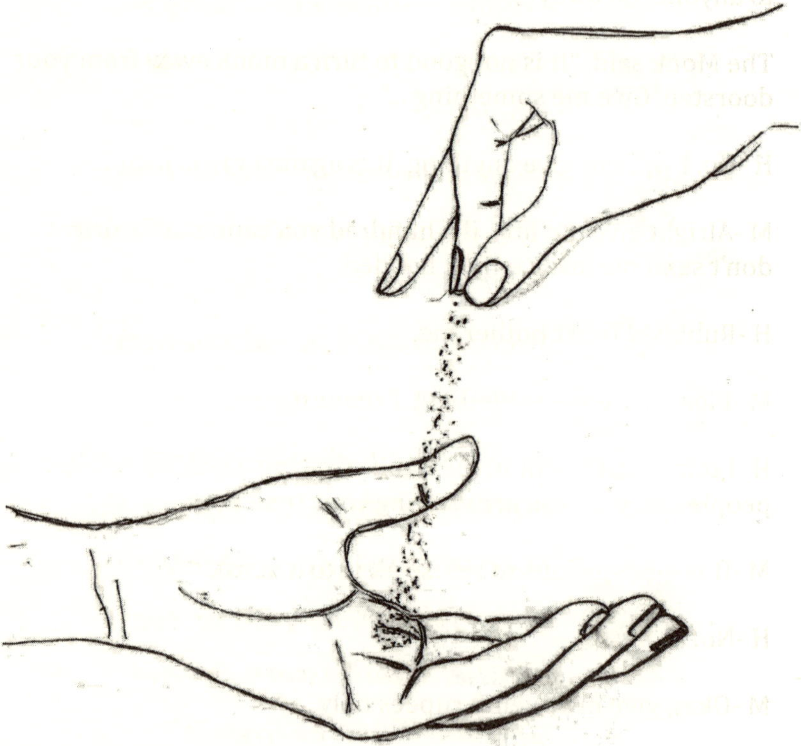

This story was narrated by Sh. M.L. Khattar, The Chief Minister of Haryana, who presided over the book launch ceremony of our sixth book, 'Sunrays for Friday'. During his address he narrated this story and suggested that it be considered as a seed for the next book. Resultantly, here it is in 'Sunrays for Saturday'!

A monk knocked at the door of a householder and begged for alms. He said, "Please give me a hundred rupees, I am in dire need." The householder, refused saying, "I don't give anything to anyone. Go away!"

The Monk said, "It is not good to turn a monk away from your doorstep. Give me something ..."

H -No, I will not give anything. It is against my principles.

M -Alright give me fifty, if a hundred you cannot afford. But don't send me away empty handed.

H -Rubbish! Don't bother me.

M -Please give me something. I request you.

H -I told you, I'm not in the habit of giving anything to lazy people like you. You are wasting your time here.

M -It is inauspicious to refuse alms to a monk.

H -No!

M -Okay, give me twenty rupees only.

H -How dare you bargain with me? I am surprised at your impudence. Why don't you go away?

M -Alright, give me just ten rupees.

H -Not a penny shall I give.

M -Don't do this. God has given you so much. Ten rupees won't make any difference to your pocket.

H -No way. Just buzz off. Don't waste my time and yours.

M -Five rupees? It's not good to turn away a needy man from your doorstep. Five rupees is all I ask for.

H- Nothing doing. Go away before I throw you out.

M -One rupee is all I ask for. Don't refuse brother. You are blessed to have so many bounties. Don't say no.

H -How stubborn you are! I said No! And no means no!

M -Alright then, do you have a fire at your hearth?

H -Yes, I do.

M -Give me a pinch of ash from your log fire.

H -Why? What will you do with it?

M -I shall not do anything with it, except dust it off my hand. But perhaps if you give something, you shall realize the joy of giving, even if all that you give is a pinch of ash!

The man still did not seem to be willing to give even a pinch of ash. The Monk continued, "And if you do not have even a pinch of ash to give, surely you would have a palm full of water ... in that case go and drown yourself in it!" (In Hindi we say, "Chullu bhar paani mein doob mar!") What an insult!

The joy of giving far outdoes the joy of receiving. Offer some food to a hungry man or even a glass of water to a thirsty man and experience the blessings and love that come your way. Bhagwan Baba says, "It is in giving that we receive."

3

Prahlad's Lineage

"Though the Earth is one, the plants vary depending upon the seeds sown. The womb of the mother symbolises Mother Earth. As is the seed of thought sown in it, so is the fruit that it yields. So, the mother should foster good thoughts, words and deeds. Only then can she beget virtuous children."

Narayan!
Narayan!

It is usually said that good souls are born into families with sacred thoughts. And evil souls are attracted to and, hence, born in homes where piety and love for God are missing. Paradoxically Prahlad was born to Hrinyakshyapu. Ever wondered why?

It is said that Hrinyakshyapu was so obsessed with the thought that he was God, and that no other supreme being existed that he would get very angry if anyone mentioned the name of Narayan in his presence. He once went for penance to the forest, to acquire *siddhis* (powers attained by gaining control over the body and the mind).

When he started to meditate under a tree, a parrot perched on the branch above him sang, "Narayan, Narayan ..." Hrinyakshyapu tried his best to concentrate but could not. He tried to shoo away the bird, but the bird flew around a bit, and came to sit on one of the branches and started chanting again, "Narayan, Narayan ..." Exasperated after many efforts, he went to a hill-top to meditate.

A short while later, the parrot came there and started off, "Narayan, Narayan, Narayan ..." Hrinyakashyapu was enraged. He glared at the parrot and shouted at it to go away. But the parrot determinedly continued to sing the name of Lord Narayan.

At his wit's end, the man found a cave to meditate in. No sooner than he started, he heard the familiar sound of "Narayan, Narayan ..." He went wild! Oh! The parrot was following him wherever he went. Utterly disgusted, he went back to the palace. The queen was surprised to see him return so soon. She was a God-loving woman who had always tried hard to reform her evil husband. Never before had he returned so soon from such a meditative stint. She wondered what had happened.

Initially, he didn't tell her why he came back, but as she repeatedly showed her concern for his well-being, he melted a little and said, "A parrot disturbed me every time I started to meditate. He kept on repeating, "Narayan, Narayan ..." I changed places several times to get him off my back but he followed me everywhere. There was no way he would stop, so I decided to come back."

The queen was inwardly very happy. She told him that she was very intrigued by this and asked him to tell her exactly what happened. So, he repeated the entire story again. In this way, he repeated the word 'Narayan' several times. She asked him, "My dear, how can a parrot speak like a human? Tell me exactly how he spoke..." So, he mimicked the parrot saying, "Narayan, Narayan..." A short while later, she said, "I am so amazed that a parrot could sing like this." So saying, she chanted the name in a different style and intonation. He corrected her, chanting the way the parrot had. In this way, the queen made her husband repeat the name of the Lord several times. Resultant to the solace she offered to him, they came closer and closer. That night, the queen conceived.

The moment in time that the child was conceived, both of them were in thoughts of Narayan. So, could the child have been anything less than a devotee of Narayan? The story has a great significance. If our thoughts are pure, at the time of conception, pure and pious souls shall be attracted to be born through us. Otherwise...

Swami once mentioned, "Aryamba was a paragon of virtues. She spent all her time in the contemplation of God and in undertaking noble deeds. As a result, Shankaracharya was born to her. Shankaracharya could become Jagadguru (world teacher) because of his mother's virtuous thoughts."

4

The Watermelons of Parra

"You received all these precious gifts from society. Have any one of you, young men and women, thought of showing gratitude to the society from which you got the name and fame? What service are you rendering to the society in return for the good things received?"

Manohar was a young boy who lived in the Parra village in Goa that is famous for its watermelons. Every year at the end of the harvest season in the last week of May, the farmers would contribute some watermelons and organise a watermelon-eating contest for the village children, wherein they could eat as much as they wanted. The children were told to spit out the seeds and not chew them.

Manohar grew up and went to IIT Mumbai. He came back after almost seven years. The childhood memory of the watermelon contest was so potent in his mind that he went out to the market to buy some watermelons.

He was disappointed and surprised at the small size available. He looked around for large watermelons but found none. Further enquiry yielded that the large variety had vanished from the market and was not to be found anywhere. Disappointed, he went in search of the head farmer who used to conduct these competitions.

He came to know that the farmer was no more and his son had taken over. He was continuing the ritual of holding the contest, but the melons offered to the kids were of small size. He had realised that the large watermelons fetched a better price at the marketplace. So, he sent the best ones for sale and kept the smaller ones for the contest. So, the best seeds were probably going to the consumers and, hence, down the drain. The seeds available now were of the substandard ones. In watermelons, the generation is just one year. Resultantly, in six-seven years, the best watermelons of Parra village were wiped out.

This is what most of us do. We keep the best for ourselves. When it comes to sharing, we give substandard stuff. This is not what our Indian culture and tradition talks of. We are a race that treats the guest as God. We are a race that sees God in everyone, even a beggar. We talk of 'Daridra Narayan'. We need to seriously work on regaining our lost value system, otherwise another fifty years hence, there will be no one, who can even throw light on what India's rich value-system has been!

Incidentally, Manohar in the story grew up to be Manohar Parrikar (currently Chief Minister of Goa). While narrating this story, he made a very thought-provoking addition to it. He said, unlike watermelons, in humans, the generations change every 25 years or so. It will probably take us 200 years to realise what we are doing to destroy the DNA of our children. The moral fibre that we Indians have been known for is fast being eroded. The factors responsible are many and cannot be listed here due to paucity of space.

Shri. Parrikar went on to say that unless we attract our best people into the teaching profession, to groom and mentor our next generation, we are in for exactly what happened to the watermelons. Of all the professions in the world, that of the teacher is the most estimable. The teacher has to impart to the students what is good and ennobling. This should be developed in all educational institutions.

Baba says, "You are born in society, you grow in society, and earn name and fame in society. You learn many skills from the society and develop intelligence, and, thereby, you gain reputation for being intelligent. You received all these precious gifts from society. Have any one of you, young men and women, thought of showing gratitude to the society from which you got the name and fame? How are you expressing your gratitude to society? And as an expression of one's gratitude, one should render selfless service to the society. It is one's foremost duty."

5

Paper Planes

"Be the master of your behaviour; do not be led away by the impulse of the moment; be conscious always of what is good for you. Carry on your daily tasks so that you do not make others suffer or suffer yourself. That is the sign of intelligent living. Train your ears to listen quietly to good and maintain your composure. Be calm and unruffled and collected (satwic)."

CIVIL PROCEDURE CODE

College had just begun after the summer break. New admissions had taken place in the first year of the five-year integrated law degree course. The freshers were in class for the first time. Some were serious kids, others naughty, while some were just tired or bored.

A young professor at a college of law had just started his lecture. He was giving them an introduction to the Civil Procedure Code of India. He had his back turned to the class as he wrote something on the white board with a marker. Just then a swift paper plane landed on his ear.

The professor turned around with brows raised. He decided to ignore the prank and returned back to his writing on the board. Zip! Along came another one that landed on his shoulder now. He turned to the class and said, "Who is that?" Everyone looked innocently at each other. The class was silent. Despite repeated questioning, no one owned up.

So, the professor said, "Alright, since you are not in the mood to study today, let's chat."

He sat informally on a desk and crossed one leg over the other. He then asked, "Let's get to know each other. My favourite hobby is travelling. I love to see new places. Tell me about yourselves. Do you guys like to travel?" "Yes!" came most of the voices in chorus. So, they talked about travelling by car and train and plane. Discussions stretched from holidaying in London to Las Vegas and Kashmir to Kerala. There were excited inputs from back-packing to trekking to group tours for river rafting and snorkeling too. Everyone got involved and many interesting travel stories were narrated. The entire mood of the class was chirpy and bubbly.

The professor said, "You know, last week when I flew here to Delhi, I took the early morning flight from Mumbai. I happened to meet the pilot of our flight just after we landed. I was so impressed with her! She was a lovely girl and we had a lot in common. We became friends and I am meeting her for dinner tonight. I asked her how she chose to become a pilot. She said that as a kid, she and her kid brother used to make paper planes and fly them. That childhood play became an obsession and then a profession for her. Her brother, however, decided to do law. She told me that he is studying in our college. She did tell me his name, but somehow it's slipped my mind. She said I could easily know who he was, because he still has a penchant for flying paper planes."

Instantly, all eyes turned towards the boy who had thrown the Paper plane at the professor. The boy blushed crimson red!

The professor put both his hands on the boy's shoulders and said, "Bro, I am beginning to grey, and my crop of curly hair did not fade just by standing in the sun. I want you to know that I'm the boss here and don't you ever forget it ..."

Well! Conventional ways of teaching and handling the youth sometimes fall short. Teachers have to innovate constantly to influence young minds. The youth are full of naughty ideas. Disciplining them requires presence of mind, intelligence and wit too!

Kids today are smart. If the teachers have to groom them, they have to be oversmart!

6

Moong Sprouts

"One discipline every one of you must heed is the control of the senses. If you give them free rein, they will drag you into calamity."

Bhagwan Baba always stressed upon the relentless practice of *sadhana* to discipline the mind and to develop moral and mental strength. He often used to visit the school hostels in his Puttaparthi School. One day he visited the boys' hostel at lunch time and asked to see what the boys were being given. Amongst the regular menu of rice, *sambar,* vegetable and *roti* were sprouted moong grains.

Swami asked the warden what it was and also took a few to taste. As he chewed it, he grimaced, not liking the taste. The boys giggled as they saw Swami make a face at the unpalatable taste of the sprouts. The boys had always hated having them. But the warden insisted that they must. Finally, it seemed the days of the sprouts were numbered. This was going to be the beginning of the end of the daily sprout battle. The boys waited with bated breath to hear Swami, tell the warden to stop giving this unpalatable stuff to the boys.

He looked at the warden and asked, "Why do you give this to them?" The warden replied, "Swami, this is sprouted moong dal and it's very rich in protein and fibre. We give it to them raw, because it's very good for them to have it in this form."

Swami said, "Is it really good for them?" "Yes, Swami!" replied the warden knowingly. "How much do you give them everyday?" "One teaspoon Swami," he gushed. "In that case, make it two teaspoons from now on!"

The boys were left gaping. What was this? Two spoons of the torturous sprouts! Swami! Why are you doing this to us? Swami smiled enchantingly and moved on. Totally unpredictable are the ways of the Lord!

The anecdote centres around sprouts, but the lesson in it runs deeper. Swami told the boys by this little incident that if something is good for you, you must take it, whether you like it or not. The way to teach self-discipline and resilience is to put yourself up to doing things you do not like to do. One normally wants to do the easier things in life, but they are not what make us strong.

Junk food like pizzas and burgers may taste yummy, but they are not really good for us. One has to train the mind to accept that tests are the taste of life. Gold shines only after being in the fire for some time, till then its impurities don't burn away.

Swami says, "Devotion, wisdom or action (*Bhakti, Jnana* or *Karma*), must all lead to the achievement of equanimity; otherwise, they are simply a sham. The curbing of the mind will take you to the winning post."

Let us take another example: when an animal is tethered to a post, it will not be able to go to another place and spoil it. It will not be able to show anger or violence or do harm to any person. But if it is untied and let loose, it can roam over various fields, destroy the crops and cause loss and harm to others. For the mischief it does, it gets beaten. Similarly, the mind must be bound by certain regulations and limits. As long as one lives within certain limits and disciplines, as well as particular rules and regulations, one will be able to maintain a good name and lead a happy and useful life.

Truly the one who can control the mind, is the winner. It is discipline in the formative years that is able to mould the child into becoming a good human being. Mind control and sense control are of utmost importance! Discipline is surely the mark of intelligent living!

7

Bhoori and Meeni

"Prema is not an illusion; it is a reality and actuality for those who have realised oneness in life."

Our father Justice M.M. Punchhi would often tell us stories about his childhood, of which he had very vivid memories. He loved cows and always kept some, so we got cow's milk all through our growing years. He once told us of a particular pair of cows, in his village in Pakpattan (now in Pakistan), called Bhoori and Meeni, who were always together. They were placed in the cowshed next to each other. They were milked one after the other, they grazed together, drank water together... Strangely a thin rope of about eight metres was tied such that one of its ends was tied to the necks of each of them.

Watching them grazing, he asked the cowherd why he had tied the rope in such a way. The cowherd asked him to watch the pair as they grazed. It seems that Bhoori always walked a step ahead and Meeni followed. If Bhoori strayed towards the left, Meeni would do so too. When Bhoori strayed further away, Meeni followed instinctively. Later, Bhoori sat down to rest in the shade and so did Meeni. The communication was perfect. Was there any language?

The cowherd said, "Watch closely Madan. Meeni is blind. It follows the smell of Bhoori and is further guided by rope." "Doesn't the rope ever break? Doesn't either of them tug at it?" asked Madan, wide eyed. "No," said the cowherd. "Bhoori understands that if she tugs at the rope and it breaks, Meeni would be left helpless. There is an instinctive sense of responsibility in Bhoori. We have never had to change the rope." "And what about, Meeni? Doesn't she ever want to run off?" "No," smiled the cowherd, "Meeni knows her limitations, she never tugs. She knows that if she breaks away, she will be alone like an orphan."

Madan asked, "How do you know this? Do you know the language of the cows?" The cowherd put his arm around little Madan's shoulders and said, "Yes and No!" Seeing the questioning look on Madan's face, he continued, "Yes, because there is only one language — the language of the heart. We can all learn it if only we want to. No, because I'm not a cow, so I don't know their alphabet!" he said grinning.

There is goodness and kindness in the animals too for those who are in need of help. Wonder why man sometimes seems to forget, that he too has a heart that beats. As Mark Twain said, "Kindness is a language which the deaf can hear and the blind can see."

Bhagwan Baba tells us, "The world is one vast society. Every individual in it is part of this society, bound to it by the love that draws an individual to another, to be kith and kin. This love is there, deep in the heart of every individual. Only it is unrecognised, ignored, doubted, denied and argued away. It is the secret source of all empathy and service. It creates the urge to live in and for society. It is Universal Love (Vishwa-Prema) that flows from one spark of the Divine to all sparks. When the eyes shine illumined by the highest wisdom, Jnana, they see all as One. Then the individual realises — *Sarvam Brahmamayam Jagath* (All is pervaded by Divinity in this apparently changing and transforming world)."

8

Importance of Documentation

"Be clear and content. Be moderate and wise. Be vigilant and steady."

Here is an anecdote shared by someone in a group of friends. Don't know if it is true, but very thought-provoking indeed...

Trains are one of the most commonly used means of transport by the public. Aaron was travelling by train to a nearby town. As he opened his laptop to catch up on his work, he loosened his neck tie to ease his tired neck. Oh! Office attire could sometimes be so uncomfortable in the heat.

A very beautiful girl sat on the seat opposite to Aaron. She was quite well dressed. They exchanged a few admiring glances. The girl smiled at him. He smiled back. A few smiles later, the girl got up and sat on the seat next to Aaron. A few minutes of awkward silence followed. But the undercurrents were potent.

Then the girl smiled sweetly and whispered, "Give me all your money, credit cards and mobile phone. Do it quietly for if you raise your voice, I will scream and tell everyone that you misbehaved with me."

The boy looked blank. After a moment of contemplation, he smiled back at her and took out a pen and paper from his pocket. He wrote, "Hi! I am deaf and dumb. I cannot hear what you said. But I can tell that you would like us to be friends. So, if you write down whatever you would like to say, we can chat!"

The girl took the pen from his hand and wrote down just what she had said a few minutes back.

The boy took the paper and carefully placed his laptop aside. He stood up and cleared his throat. He spoke loud enough for all to hear, "Hello everyone! May I have your attention please? Allow me to read out this message from this lovely young lady here."

Surely you can tell what the position of the girl would be now. The presence of mind of the boy saved him not only his money, credit cards and phone, but also saved him from character assassination.

Well!!! That is the importance of documentation, common sense and presence of mind! Common sense they say is seldom common ... Do think about it!

Reflecting on this, I am saddened by the state of our society today. How easy it is for an innocent person to get into trouble if he is not on guard at all times? How gullible and prone to predacious elements the innocent are? But why has this happened? Why are so many children walking the wrong path? The reason for the depletion of values is that the children are not receiving the right mentoring at home and at school.

Swami says that the end of education is Character. Today, we are educating our children in the best of schools and colleges. Their IQ and EQ may be tops, but what about their values, character, common sense, sense of responsibility towards parents as well as towards the society and the Nation?

Just holding a fancy degree from a great University is not all it takes to be a good human being... there is so much more to it!

9

Too Much Sugar in the Milk

"Everyone is eager to be happy; everyone wants to work less and gain more, give little and get amply, but nobody experiments with wanting less and giving more!"

There once was a miser who prayed to Lord Krishna and said that he wanted to perform worship and rituals for the Lord, but he didn't want to spend any money doing this. Krishna told him that he didn't want anything anyways! He could simply start doing mental worship. No money would be spent this way! The Lord in His infinite mercy asked him which form of Krishna he liked. The miser said – Bala Krishna.

So, a typical day in the miser's life would be one where he would wake up early and mentally fetch a bucket of water from the river Yamuna. In his mind, he would bathe the idol of Baby Krishna. He would then ask him which colour clothes he would like to wear today. The miser would then dress Him up mentally in the said colour of dress. He would mentally make Krishna wear beautiful necklaces of diamond and gold. He would add a nice pair of earrings and bracelets and anklets. He would mentally place a small dot of *chandan tilak* on his forehead and a beautiful crown of glittering gold studded with precious stones on the head of the beautiful blue-skinned God. He would then offer him dollops of fresh butter, sweetmeats, milk, etc. He would then mentally light a lamp and incense sticks and do Aarti. *"Aarti kunj bihari ki, Sri Giridhar Krishna Murari ki..."*

This mental worship and prayer became so much of a habit, that each day the miser continued this routine for years together. So involved was he in it that he could see the little baby Krishna playing before his eyes, eating butter, drinking milk, etc.

This continued for twelve years. One day while mentally offering sweetened milk to Krishna, the miser felt that by mistake, he had added too much sugar to it. So, he tried to get the sugar out, thinking that he could put it to use elsewhere. While trying to extract the excess sugar from the milk, his love and emotions were very intense.

Krishna appeared before him in physical form. He said, "As it is, you have been performing mental worship. You have not spent a penny on the offering. How does it matter if the sugar is slightly excessive?" So saying, Krishna touched the miser on the shoulder. The very touch of Divinity transformed the miser and he became a realised soul, who instantly became detached and knowledgeable.

Truly, it's the intensity of our remembering the Lord that brings Him to us. It's our yearning that gets His attention. The Lord says that it doesn't matter how you remember Him; as long as you remember Him! There are the extreme cases like Krishna's uncle Kansa and nephew Shishupala, who had sworn enmity against Him. They remembered Him all the time, but with hatred, jealousy and enmity! He allowed them to merge into Him, because they thought of Him all the time! Who but the Lord can exhibit such benevolence?

He is always ready to connect. What matters is when you are able to connect with Him. True Devotion is concentration of the mind on God and experiencing oneness with the Divine.

Prayer must come from the depths of feeling; the Lord looks for the sincerity in your feeling *(bhava)*, not outward pomp and grandeur *(bahya)*.

Really speaking, what we witness in the world today is a great deal of play-acting. Many people declare themselves as spiritual aspirants. Every believer claims that they are connecting with God. Offering to God what God has provided is like offering to the Ganga water from the Ganga. The Lord wants the offering of love, pure hearts, good deeds ... He also accepts the offering of ego, greed, lust, etc. if we are willing to renounce them.

10

Koji – The Pup

"The obligations of parents do not end with providing food, schooling and knowledge of worldly matters. The children should also be provided with right values."

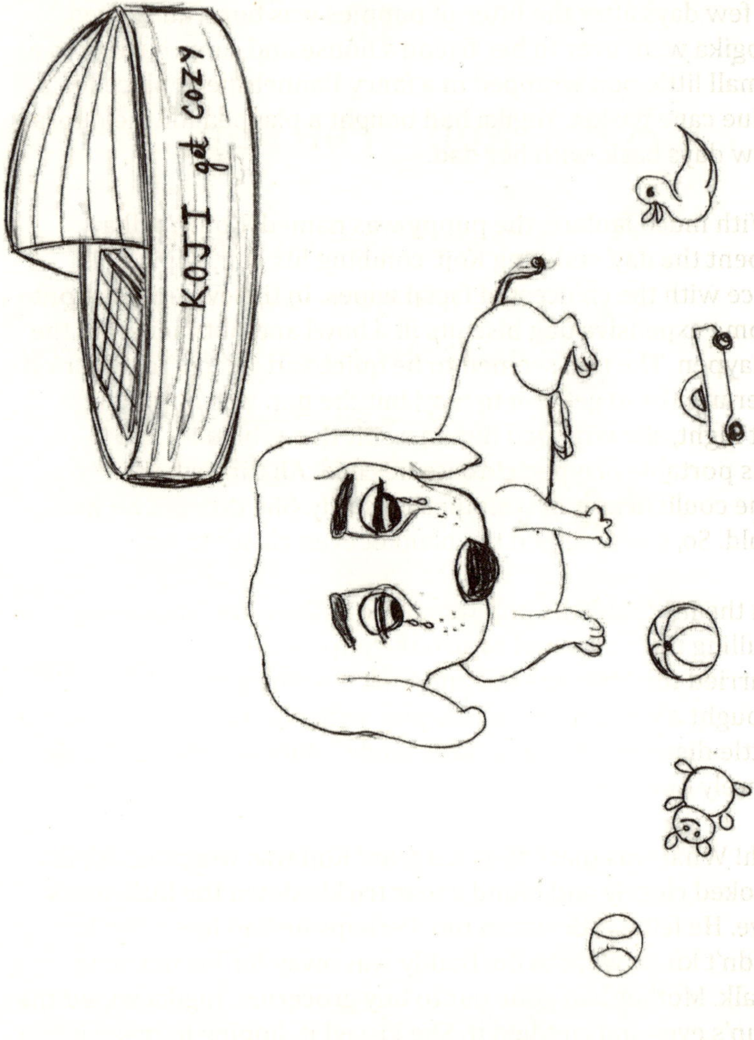
KOJI got COZY

Yogika had a friend who had a female dog that was soon to give birth to puppies. She had persuaded her father with a lot of difficulty to let her get one of the pups home.

A few days after the litter of puppies was born, an excited Yogika went over to her friend's house and came back with a small little pup wrapped in a fancy flannel sheet, placed in a blue cane basket. Yogika had bought a playpen for the pup, a few days back, with her dad.

With much fanfare, the puppy was named 'Koji'. Yogika spent the day, cuddling Koji, combing his hair, wiping his face with the choicest of facial wipes. In the evening, she put some expensive dog biscuits in a bowl and put them into the playpen. The pup seemed to be quiet and sleepy. Yogika tried her utmost to get him to play, but the pup was not interested. At night, she wrapped him in a soft fleece blanket and kept his portable playpen close to her bed. All through the night, she could hear him whimpering softly. She thought he was cold. So, she wrapped the blanket even closer to him.

In the morning, the pup was quite listless. Yogika was not willing to give up and return the pup to her friend. She carried the little one out and took it to the garden. She had bought a soft ball for him to play with. She threw the ball at a little distance and said, "Koji, fetch!" But the little pup could barely open its eyes.

Oh! What was that? Was it a tear? Koji was weeping! Yogika looked closely and found a tear trickle down the little one's eye. He felt a little warm too. Perhaps he had fever. Yogika didn't know what to do. Daddy was away for his morning walk. Mother had gone out to buy groceries. Yogika wiped the pup's eyes and cuddled it. She kissed it, hoping to make it feel better. But she felt quite helpless.

Just then, she heard mother come in. "Mama!" she cried out. "What happened, Yogika?" asked mother anxiously, seeing tears brimming in the little girl's eyes. "Koji is not well. I don't know what to do. Please help me Mama."

Mother took the pup in her arms and said, "When did you last give him milk?" Yogika looked at her wide-eyed, "Milk? Why?" Mother said, "Because that's all he's going to have for a few days. Tell me, when did you give it to him last?"

Yogika said, "Mama, I didn't give him any..."

Mother quickly filled a baby bottle with milk and gave it to the pup. He suckled it and finished it to the last drop. Soon it regained some energy...

Many of us do what Yogika did. We provide the playpen, the doggie biscuits, the warm fleece blanket and the soft ball. But we forget to provide the 'milk'. In bringing up our children, sometimes we are so enamoured by the fancy frivolities that we tend to overindulge our children. What we forget to provide is our love and our time.

What children really need is not fancy clothes and toys, nor expensive vacations and electronics. What they need is a part of you... your love, and your time. These are invaluable... they are priceless!

Baba tells us that parents today lavish too much affection on their children. But such affection alone is not enough. There should be both 'love' and 'law'. Only when both love and restraint are present will the love prove beneficial. For all the evil habits of children, who are naturally innocent, the parents are primarily responsible. Parents have to make sure that they teach proper values and behaviour to the children.

11

Intoxicating Water

"Just as while eating you reject bad food, you must reject bad thoughts and take in only good and wholesome thoughts into the mind. Do not bear any ill-will towards those who may have done some harm to you."

HIC!

The Mayor of the city had gone out for a trip. In his absence, a wicked man mixed something in the water reservoir such that all the water that was being supplied to all the houses was laced with a drug that caused people to behave like lunatics. In a day or two, the behaviour of everyone became weird.

People roamed the streets, screaming, dancing and abusing. Young girls and women roamed around in the day and night half-clad, their hair open and unkempt, their faces layered with war paint. The whole city was awake even at night. Loud music played. People zipped around on bikes or in cars unmindful of traffic rules. Mothers left their children crying while they danced and ran around in a crazy fashion passing lewd comments.

Everyone went mad. The worst part was that no one could point it out because everyone had gone mad, so no one was aware of what had happened.

People were painting their hair in weird shades of orange and blue. They were painting images of snakes and scorpions on their arms and chests. They were eating and drinking at all times, unmindful of whether it was night or day.

People lay on the streets to sleep when they got fagged out. Babies were crying but the mothers were too drunk to care.

Then, one day the mayor came back. He was horrified at what he saw. He tried to shake people up and bring them back to their senses, but they all thought that the Mayor had gone mad. So, they called him names and even threatened to remove him from the post and disgrace him publically. The Mayor sat down, deep in thought. He tried to understand what had happened. What was the common element that all of them could have been exposed to except air and water? And then he realised... Yes! It must be the water! So, he went to check out the town water reservoir and sure enough, he found a can of intoxicant lying there. He drained the entire tank and cleaned it personally. He then allowed it to fill up with fresh and clean water. In a day or two, people started returning to their senses.

Dear reader, please pause here for a minute! Read carefully...

Isn't this what the state of our society is today? People are behaving as if they are under the influence of an intoxicant. What is needed is a 'Mayor' who chops off the free supply of intoxicants, drugs, narcotics and even access to too much on the Internet. The free and easy availability of adult content on the Internet is poisoning our children's innocent minds. It is no less than an intoxicant or a dangerous drug. Youth is the stage in life when the mind is soft and impressionable. Sometimes people don't even realise that they are on the wrong track till someone physically shakes them back to their senses.

Dear parents! Do keep an eye on your children. Be informed of what they are doing. Our future and the future of the Nation, of humanity depends on how our children shape up!

Everything that we consume through the senses, whether it is food, water, air, thoughts, ideas, music, movies, etc, affects our minds. So, let's be careful of everything that we allow in ... To everything that is pollutant, just shut your doors and tell it to keep out!

12

Respect for Each Other

"In the family, cultivate patience
and mutual respect;
in the community, have
righteousness
and justice."

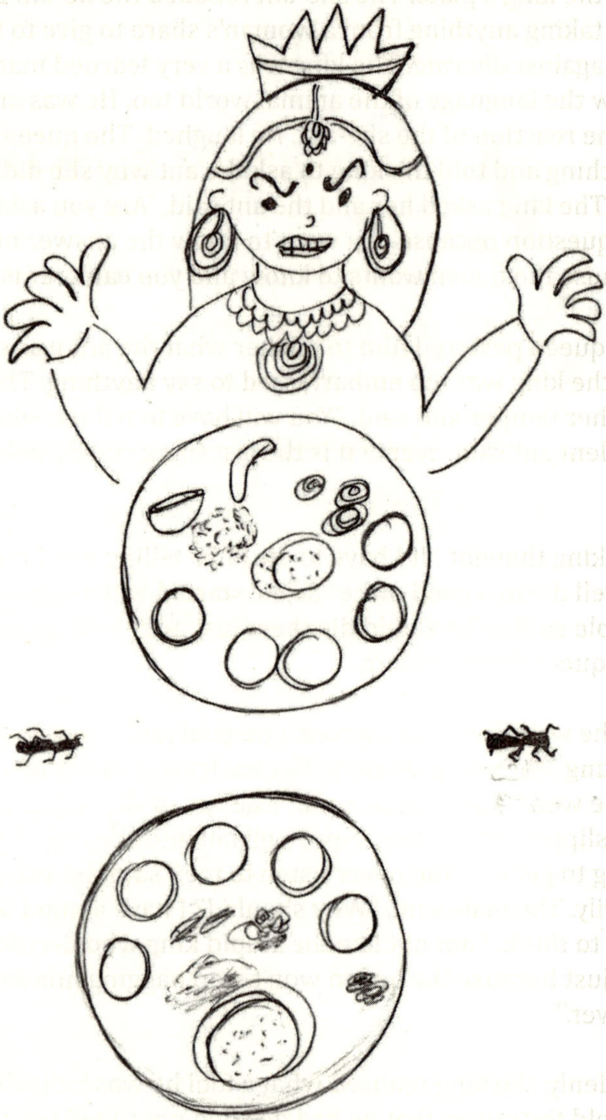

A king and a queen were having dinner when a male ant picked up a grain of food from the queen's plate and put it into the king's plate. The she-ant rebuked the he-ant saying that taking anything from a woman's share to give to the man was against *dharma*. The king was a very learned man who knew the language of the animal world too. He was amused by the reaction of the she-ant. He laughed. The queen too was watching and told the king to ask the ant why she did as she did. The king asked her and the ant said, "Are you asking me the question because you want to know the answer or just because the queen wants to know and you can't refuse her?"

The queen pestered him to tell her what the ant was saying, but the king was too embarrassed to say anything. The queen lost her temper and said, "You will have to tell me what this insolent ant said, even if it is the last thing you do before you die."

The king thought, 'If I have to die after telling her, I might as well die in a good place.' So, he started walking towards, temple so that he would die there just after telling the queen. The queen followed him.

On the way, they came across a he-goat and a she-goat fighting. The she-goat said, "Get me fresh grass from the rim of the well." The he-goat said, "The rim of the well is slimy and slippery. If my foot slips I will fall into the well. I am not going to get it." "You never listen to me," said the she-goat angrily. The male said, "Why should I? I have a mind of my own to think. I am not like the stupid king who decides to die, just because the queen won't stop nagging him for an answer."

Suddenly, the king realised what a fool he was behaving like. He told the queen that he had decided not to tell her the answer of the ant. Come what may!

Even the queen had to give up her abstinence. In marital relationships, it is good to care for the other feeling's. Respect for each other is important. But making a fool of the other person for ego satisfaction is ridiculous. The home, the workplace and the society are all the training grounds of tolerance. The relationship with each other must be based on love and respect, not fear. Only the atmosphere of love and respect can guarantee happy and cordial relations.

13

The Sweat of Your Brow

"The body is the temple of the Lord; keep it in good and strong condition."

A young man of about twenty years had put on a lot of weight. He tried many ways to lose it but nothing seemed to work.

One day a wise man visited his house. He said, "Son, I will give you a powder. Mix it in the sweat of your brow and make a paste. Apply it all over the fatty areas of your body. Your weight will melt. I guarantee it. Here, take this pouch. It should be enough for a month. After that, you can come to me. I shall give you some more. And just for this month, say 'no' to all fried food and sweet food."

The young fellow ran all day and collected the sweat from his brow in a little container. With a lot of difficulty, he had enough to make a paste with the powder. He smeared it on to his tummy, etc. and rubbed it well.

He did this religiously for a month. To his sheer delight, he lost a good amount of weight. Elated he went to the wise man and asked him for some more powder. The old man said simply, "Son, what did you do to collect the sweat from your brow?"

The boy said, "I ran six kilometres, and kept collecting the sweat." The wise man said, "So, continue to run six kilometres. That's all. I only gave you some holy ash. The running has made you lose weight. When all you did earlier was laze around and eat junk food, it was natural that you would gain weight. You have to remember always that you have to burn what you eat. In your case, you have to burn more than you eat, to burn up the stocks you have kept in reserve!!!"

Many people think that the human body is just for 'eat, drink and be merry!' Their day revolves around food, food and food. Obesity is a disease that plagues a lot of youngsters today. It all bogs down to junk food, over-eating and laziness. Sedentary life-styles are unhealthy lifestyles. Don't be a couch potato or a sofa lizard.

The general tendency of youngsters today is to prefer junk food over the healthier options. The parents need to impress upon children the importance of healthy living. Eating healthy and playing in the open is something the younger generation seems to have no preference for. Why is it that our children want to play digital games and not real games? Why is it that they want to play in air conditioned arcades and not outside in the fresh air? A sound mind can dwell only in a healthy body.

Our body is a temple if we think of it to be one. The body is not just a mass of flesh and bones. It is a sacred instrument earned after many births of Sadhna. It is equipped with reason and emotion, and is capable of being used for deliverance from grief and evil. We must honour it as such; keep it in good condition so that it might serve that high purpose. We should maintain it even more carefully than the brick and mortar houses we live in, and always preserve the conviction that it is a divine instrument. We should use it for that pure purpose for which it has been designed and gifted to us.

It is important to eat healthy food. Everything, including fried food and sweets, can be eaten, but in moderation. Basically, if disease sets in after unhealthy eating, then we have to resort to medicines. Sometimes we see that people need to take lots of medicines. Why should medicine be our food when food itself can be our medicine? We should eat to live, not just live to eat.

14

Because of Sandalwood

"Every action, howsoever small or trivial, has its reaction. Good actions earn good returns. Bad actions result in bad consequences."

BEST QUALITY SANDALWOOD

A king and a rich merchant were very good friends. For a long time, the merchant who dealt in sandalwood was not doing well. The wood being so costly had hardly any takers. So, business was slow. There was hardly any earning.

One day he noticed that there was termite attacking some of the wood in the storehouse. He was very upset. He started to rack his brains about how to find a buyer who could buy the wood in bulk.

A thought crossed his mind. If the king were to die, surely sandalwood would be used in large quantities for his pyre. That should solve his problem. Otherwise his trade was doomed.

Interestingly, around the same time, the king was strategising with his ministers about how to increase the wealth in the coffers. It came to his mind that if the merchant (who was actually his friend) died, all his riches would come to the treasury because he had no issue.

A day or two later, the king was meditating and he realised what an evil thought his mind had cooked up. Because he loved his friend so much, he sent for him and told him about his thoughts and apologised for sinning in thought.

The merchant, too, then told him about his thoughts, which were around the same time. Both were stunned at each other's revelation.

The king became very pensive. After a while, he said, "My friend, why didn't you wish that I would buy all your sandalwood to make sandalwood doors for the palace? Or that I should get made a beautiful *jhoola* for Lord Krishna with intricate carvings from an accomplished sandalwood artist?"

Isn't it uncanny? One person thinks ill of another and similar thoughts emerge in other's minds too. It's like a mirror image. Our thoughts float into the cosmos and reach places. What goes round definitely comes around. If you give love, you get love. If you give goodness, you get back goodness. But if all that you can disperse is bitterness, hatred, negativity... what will you get? You can only gather what you scatter. You get only what you give!

All that we experience in the outside world is only a reaction, reflection and resound of our inner being. We are, however, deluded to think that this reaction, reflection and resound is independent of us. Whatever feeling comes out of your heart and takes a shape outside is the form you see. It means that that form has already been conceived by you.

We have to learn to keep the mind and the intellect serene and sacred, free from dirt. When thoughts and feelings are impure and agitated, we cannot be calm and happy.

When the mind is polluted, so are our reactions. To keep the mind clean, we must analyse sympathetically situations involving others and their activities, and then decide on how to react to them.

15

The Old Vest

"But always remember that they (worldly things) are transient; that the joy they give is trivial and temporary. Know their real worth; do not overestimate them. Do not develop attachment (moha) towards them."

An old man spent his life in doing good deeds, helping people, serving the needy, praying and performing all activities that would qualify for a God-loving man. He lived simply and was quite unattached to worldly things. His only attachment was to God.

He knew that he would soon be passing on. One day he told his son, "Keep this old vest of mine. My mother gave it to me. It's very dear to me. When I die, make me wear it before you cremate me." The son was quite surprised at his father's attachment to the vest. He took the vest and said, "Father, this is practically in tatters. Why don't we get you a similar new one?" But the old man said, "No, No. I like this one. Keep it safely. And don't forget. Please remember to carry out this last wish of mine."

Some days hence, while doing his morning prayers, the old man died peacefully. As per the Hindu custom, the son bathed the body and was directed to wrap it in white cotton cloth. He proceeded to put on the old vest in accordance with the last wish of the deceased father.

The Brahmin who was presiding told him that it was against the custom to wear anything, whatever it may be. The son insisted. But the Brahmin was adamant. The matter was discussed with the family elders, but they too seemed to agree with the Brahmin. The arguments went a little further. Some voices, young and old, were raised. Some terse words were exchanged. There was total chaos. The time fixed for the cremation was drawing close. What to do now? Either he would have to annoy the Brahmin and the whole clan, or he could honour the last wish of his erstwhile father. What a dilemma!

Amidst all this, a man who was the clerk of the deceased father walked up to the son and handed over to him a white envelope. It contained a letter from the deceased father. This is what it said, "My dear son, are you watching the drama? I cannot even take a tattered and worn-out vest with me. One day you too shall be in this position. All of us have to go from here, wrapped in a white cloth. We can take nothing with us. Don't run after money or riches. Never hurt another or cheat another for money. Never earn money by unscrupulous means. All our lives we run after money. In the end, everything gets left behind. All I am taking with me is the fruit of my good Karma. That shall be the case with you too. Spend your life and your money doing good deeds. Spend your money to help those in need. Be Happy ..."

This is the eternal truth for all of us. The sooner we understand it, the better. Let us work towards a better after-life, by doing good deeds, while we have the good fortune to be in human form. Let us earn grace to be secure in this life and the next!

Be in the world, but do not let the world be in you. It is the love for God and good that will be your saviour. The worldly acquisitions, wealth, family, property, etc., everything will stay here. You shall go alone.

16

Grapes Turned Sour

"Your heart should be like glass, with the spiritual light inside illuminating the world outside. The inner urges on interacting with the world outside should make one lean towards service, empathy and mutual help."

One evening a man was on his way home. He stopped by to buy fruit from a way-side fruit-seller. He picked up a bunch of grapes and asked the price. The boy said, "Eighty rupees a kg." Next to the grape bunches were lying a small heap of grapes that looked like they had been plucked off the bunch.

As the man looked across the fruit stall, his eyes spotted a little boy wearing a shabby-looking shirt looking at the grapes with craving eyes. The boy offered a crumpled five-rupee note to the fruit-seller and pointed at the loose grapes. The seller gave him a handful. The man thought that what he had given to the boy must weigh at least a hundred grams. He asked the fruit-seller, "What is the rate of those?" The seller said, "Those are forty rupees a kilo." "What is the difference between the two?" enquired the man. "Nothing sir, except that these have fallen off from the bunch, so I am selling them at half price."

Just then the boy who had already started eating the grapes from the little packet said, "Uncle, these grapes are sour. Don't buy them." The grape-seller looked at the boy with a frown. The man picked up one grape from the heap and put it into his mouth. It was quite sweet. He looked at the boy and asked, "This is quite nice. Why did you say that these grapes are sour?"

The boy said sheepishly, "Sir, if you buy these, what will we buy?"

The man was dumb-founded. He realised that the poor boy could only afford the grapes because they were cheaper now. Had they been at the original price, he could not have afforded to buy them.

Sometimes, we tend to overlook these small things.

The government arranges food grain, oil, sugar, cooking gas, etc. at subsidised prices for the poor. Sometimes these benefits are misused by the rich. In the state of Punjab, the government gave free electricity to the poor farmers. Effectively, all the rich landlords who were farmers by vocation were using that electricity and thereby, swindling the government.

Sometimes subsidies are provided for a purpose. If they are not meant for us, let us not try to grab them and take undue advantage. Let us not be selfish.

Pause a moment to think about this — Despite the striking progress in the fields of science and technology, there has been deterioration in morals and social behaviour because of the growth of selfishness. Self-interest is predominant in every action. If one's entire life is governed by selfishness, what happens to the society? Every individual has a responsibility to the society from which he derives so many benefits. Society is based on the principle of mutual give and take.

A man without the basic human values of love, duty, empathy, sympathy, etc. is verily an animal. He is not fit to be called a man. If the haves do not empathise with the have-nots, it is a very sorry state of affairs!

17

Ashoka's Birthday

"Where have your good old human qualities gone? Truth, tolerance, morality, discipline — when would you accept them? Arise, awake! Establish the Kingdom Divine (Rama-Rajya), resplendent with mansions of truth, right conduct, and peace. Remember and learn from the rule of divine personages, and their characteristics. Quench the burning flames of ignorance, peacelessness, injustice, and envy with the waters of love, forbearance and truth. Love your fellow brethren. Develop the feeling of mutuality."

Indian history tells of many iconic kings. Emperor Ashoka, was one such king. Every year on his birthday, his subordinate kings would assemble and give gifts at his court and he would give gifts to them in return.

This time on his birthday, all the kings had assembled in the capital. One of them said, "Oh virtuous king! I have good news for you. This year I have collected three times the revenue of the previous years and I offer it to you as a gift!" The king smiled.

The next king said, "My Lord! This year we have grossly reduced the salaries of the employees and cut down on public expenditure in a big way. Resultantly, I have brought six times the amount I have been paying in previous years. Please accept it as my gift to you!" The king nodded.

The third king said, "Mercy my Lord! The monsoon has failed this year. There have been very meagre crops. My farmers don't have enough even to feed their families. Please forgive me. I have nothing to offer, this year." As the king hung his head down, Ashoka looked at him benevolently.

The next king, said, "Your Majesty, we have had to deal with rebellion and revolt within the provinces. Many a head had to be quietened. With a lot of difficulty, we have been able to bring peace and stability to the province. This is the only gift I can offer to you. Revenue collection has not been possible in the strife-torn state."

The king smiled and half closed his eyes, as if trying to understand and absorb the lesson of peace and distress alternatively.

Last in line was the king of Magadha. He said, "Oh Mighty Emperor! I have collected huge amounts of tax from my people, but, have spent it all in building hospitals and schools, wells and guest houses. I got tanks dug, store wells too. My people now have clean drinking water all the year round.

Trees have been planted along all roads to provide shade to travellers. The public officials are well paid, so they conduct their duties with zest and zeal. All public monies collected have been spent for the benefit of the people. My people are happy. I offer the love, peace and the well-being of my people, to you on your birthday." The Emperor stood up and embraced the king. He gave him the choicest of gifts, much more valuable than those given to others.

Money is not the be-all and end-all of everything. Surely taxes have to be collected for a country to function, but the well-being and progress of the people is so important too.

The Almighty Lord too is happy when you care for the well-being of others. Bhagwan Baba always guided us to feel the pain of others and work for the benefit of the underprivileged. Not only did He guide us to work for others, but also to pray for others, by reciting everyday, the prayer for Universal peace — *"Samasta Loka Sukhino Bhavantu,"* which means, 'May all the beings, of all the worlds be happy!'

18

Sleeping on the Seashore

"Never judge others by their external appearance or by words alone. In fact, no test of human qualities is more stringent than the examination of the work one does."

Walking along the seaside on the sandy beach, a saint was enjoying the cool mist-laden breeze as it played with his open hair and flowing beard. He was waiting for the sun to rise, for watching the sun emerge like a fireball out of the shining sea was always a beautiful sight to behold. Just then he saw a young lad of about twenty sleeping on the sand with his head in the lap of a woman. The pallu of her saree partially covered his face. There was an empty bottle of liquor lying next to them.

The saint was disgusted at the very idea of the man drinking, that too in the wee hours of the morning. He thought to himself, 'These drunkards don't even see what time of the day it is. Dawn or Brahma Muhurtam is supposed to be most auspicious for prayer. Tch!Tch!' To add to it, he was sleeping with his head in the lap of the woman. How shameless! And how undignified to be in this position in a place where anyone and everyone can see! Display of lust in such a place! How uncouth! The saint looked away distastefully and hastened to walk further ahead to remove them from his sight.

A few minutes later, he heard a voice from the sea screaming, "Help! Help! I'm drowning."

The saint could only look on helplessly, because he did not know how to swim. Just then he saw that the young lad had snapped out of his slumber and was racing towards the drowning man. In a jiffy, he was in the water and a few deft strokes of his strong arms were all it took to reach the man who was gasping for breath. In a few minutes, the lad brought the man back to safety and pressed his lungs to expel the water therein.

The saint was watching from a distance and wondered whether he could still brand the lad to be a shameless, impudent fellow. Confused at his thoughts, he decided to go up to the lad and clarify his doubts. The saint asked him, "Who are you? I thought you were drunk when I first saw you." The young fellow bowed respectfully to the saint and said, "I am a fisherman. I had been out at sea all day and night. I came back to the shore at around 4 AM. My mother had been waiting for me at the shore. She had brought food and some water for me in this old glass bottle.

I was so exhausted when I reached the shore that I just had the food and the whole bottle of water and lay down on the sand. The cool breeze of the sea fanned me so beautifully that I dozed off. My mother lifted my head and placed it on her lap.

The saint had no words now. Truly, what meets the eye may not always be real. It is best not to judge others. Who knows what the truth is?

In a discourse, Swami said, "You will soon come to the conclusion that there are far more useful ways of spending the little time you have here in this life than ridiculing or praising others. Do not concern yourself with the faults and excellences of others. Instead care earnestly and sincerely about your own faults. Foster more carefully and sincerely your own best qualities. This is my advice to you today."

19

Brats and Birds

"When there is peace in our heart, we will be able to witness peace all round. Unrest, sorrow, anger, and so on are the reaction, reflection and resound of the state of our inner being. Sorrows and difficulties, anger and unrest are of our own creation."

An old man had five married sons. His wife had died. All of them lived together in the same house. Theirs was a large house. There were many grandchildren of all ages in the house.

All day long, the house was abuzz with activity. The day would start with the toddlers crying for milk, the mothers hurrying around doing housework, and dropping the kids off to school. There were activities like yoga, singing, aerobics, guitar, chess, cricket, tuitions, homework etc. happening all day. The children and the servants would be shouting, playing and running up and down the stairs all afternoon.

The old man would try to meditate and concentrate on prayer, but due to the incessant disturbance in the house, he was unable to and this led to a lot of frustration.

One day he just left the house and went to the jungle. He found a large tree, cleared some space under it and sat down to meditate. Moments later, he felt an insect crawling on his foot. He opened his eyes to see the insect. He shook it away only to be disturbed by a bumble bee buzzing around his nose. He shook his head and waved his hands to ward it off. Minutes later, he felt a bird dropping on his head. He was at his wit's end! He got up enraged and shouted. "Brats, in the house! Beetles and bees, bugs and birds in the jungle! Where the hell should I go?"

He walked towards the village, looking for suitable place, but found none. So fed up was he that he decided to put an end to his life, thinking that he would take birth again in favourable circumstances and then continue with his *sadhna* in his next life.

He built a pyre and sat on it. He was about to light it and immolate himself, when a man shouted out and said, "If you must immolate yourself, wait a while till the wind turns its direction. If you burn yourself now, the stench shall come our way and pollute our houses. And if you are so impatient to do so just now, then pick up your pyre and shift it to another place. But do not disturb our peace."

That was the last straw! He couldn't even die in peace!

In a moment of realisation, he understood that the peace that he sought to achieve by prayer and meditation could not be achieved by changing the external situation. Changing the externals would just change the nature of the circumstances, but the real issue would remain.

Why? Because the real issue was within him! The mind has to be quietened and quelled. It has to be groomed and trained to look inwards, not outwards. It is not easy, but it's the only way. The sound of our breath is a constant reminder of who we are. Every time we breathe in, the sound 'so' and every time we breathe out, the sound 'hum' is created. 'So-hum' means — I am that. It is a constant reminder that 'I' am one with God. He and I are one. So, with every inhalation-exhalation, we are reminded of the Divinity latent in us ... yet we forget!

The mind is like a mad monkey. Swami always says, when you feel that your mind is agitated and jumps around like a mad monkey, sit down in a corner and repeat to yourself slowly, "I am not a monkey. I am a man. I am not a monkey. I am a man..."

The eye, the ear, the tongue, etc. are like wild horses that have no bridle between the teeth, unlike trained horses. We must learn one discipline — controlling of our senses. If we can do that, we can achieve a lot!

20

Do You Know How To Swim?

"Education sans wisdom, wisdom bereft of discrimination, action without discretion, erudition lacking sagacity, power not justified by credentials, statements not based on truth, music wanting in melody, adoration not sustained by devotion, a person devoid of common sense and character, a student not endowed with humility, and a discourse that fails to inspire: these serve no useful purpose. Knowledge without personal experience is futile. You should gain wisdom through experience."

A man was holidaying in a tourist beach resort, at the banks of the sea in a small township in India.

One day he asked a local boatman if he would take him for a joy ride into the sea.

The sea was calm and the little boat moved smoothly in the water as the man slathered sun tan lotion all over his body. He lay down and stretched his body as he enjoyed the salty air fanning his sun-tanned frame. He wore a funky flowered shirt, orange-coloured Bermudas, a wide jute hat and dark glasses to protect his face from the sun.

Lazily, he asked the boatman if he had a newspaper. The boatman told him that he never got one because he was illiterate. The man threw up his hands in exasperation and said, "What good is it to be alive if you can't even read? Surely a quarter of your life is as good as washed away into the sea, you unlettered goon!"

A short while later, the man asked the boatman if he had a radio. The simpleton said that he had never felt the need for one. The man laughed scornfully and said, "Oye, Oye, how ancient are you man? Which age do you live in? How can you survive in this world without having a radio or a music player to enjoy some music? So, all you do is fish around or ferry people around in this little boat! What a cocoon you live in! Come on man; at least sometimes try to know about what the rest of the world is up to. Good Lord! Without a radio, I think a quarter of your life is as good as washed away into the sea."

The man dozed off and a while later, when he got up, he wondered what time it was and asked the boatman if he had a watch. The boatman replied that he didn't ever feel the need for one. The simple man regulated his life by the rising and setting of the Sun! The man laughed and said, "Whether you need it or you don't, whether you know how to see the time in it or you don't, if you don't own a watch, a quarter of your life is as good as being washed away into the sea!"

The boatman pretended to be unaffected, as tears filled his eyes. Insult is greater than injury... Sooner than later, the sky darkened and the cool breeze turned into a nasty storm. The sea became rough and the little boat bobbled up and down dangerously, and it began to pour in sheets.

"Do you know how to swim," shouted the boatman trying to make himself heard above the roar of thunder and lightning. The man cried, "No... I don't!" "In that case, your entire life is about to be washed away into the sea," said the boatman as he tried desperately to keep the boat afloat in the raging waters.

Well! Certain things are important and others are just knowledge. It's good to be knowledgeable and educated but one has to learn to distinguish between what is most important to learn is one's life.

Everyone is placed in different circumstances in life. No two are identical. But there are certain things one must know as basic understanding. It's great to be aware about the world and what's happening around, but it's more important to arm yourself with the basics depending upon your circumstances.

Common sense they say is seldom common. On a spiritual front, devotion and faith in God are what keep you afloat in trying times in life. We as parents owe it to our children to instil in them the basic values of life and teach them how to connect with the supreme power! If parents won't, who will?

21

The Best Kind of Devotee

"No bhokta (enjoyer) can be a bhakta (devotee); that is to say, one who has an eye on the profit that can be derived from service to God cannot be a true devotee. Such people praise the Lord to the skies one day and decry Him the next when their fortune gets dry."

Our scriptures have innumerable little stories and anecdotes in them that are interesting and they make very good reading too. This is one where the Lord tells us who a good devotee is. We found this to be beautiful, so thought of sharing! Reading such material surely inspires us to also be what the Lord wants us to be...

Krishna was sitting with a group of devotees. One of them asked, "What kind of devotee is the best kind? Which one pleases you most?"

They were sitting by the riverside. Krishna did what we call 'a practical experiment'. He asked the man to fetch a pebble from the riverbed. The pebble was brought. Krishna said, "It's wet on the outside, break it and check how it is inside." So, the pebble was struck by a large stone and broken into two. The inside was dry as a bone. Krishna said, "This kind of devotee is coated with devotion only on the outside, that too only till he is in the spiritual atmosphere or in ideal conditions. The moment it is removed from those ideal conditions, it dries up even on the outside. And the inside is dry and unaffected all the while." Krishna shook His head in disapproval of such people who profess to be devotees.

Krishna smiled as the man tried to absorb what the Lord had just said. A minute later, Krishna Himself walked to the edge of the river and soaked the hem of his silken angavastram (shawl). He said, "Look, the threads of the cloth are soaked inside out. They are dripping too. This kind of devotee is totally suffused with devotion, to the point of dripping. But as soon as I come out of the water, the wind shall dry the cloth and it shall be completely devoid of all the traces of water (devotion). Most devotees are of this kind. They remain devoted only till they are surrounded by Godly activities, while they are visiting a place of worship or praying, etc. The moment they move out into the world, the devotion simply evaporates." The man was listening with rapt attention. He was grappling with his thoughts. What was Krishna coming to?

He looked questioningly at Krishna. So, who was the best devotee? He waited with bated breath for Krishna to reveal more wisdom.

Krishna smiled bewitchingly and said, "Here is a lump of sugar. Go and throw it in the river." The man did that and came back. After a minute, Krishna said, "Now bring back the lump." The man looked for it, but in vain. He couldn't find it. Krishna smiled and said, "You can't find it because it is not there anymore. It has dissolved into nothingness. This is the best kind of devotee. He loses himself into the Lord. He becomes nothing by merging into the Lord. He loses his identity to become one with the Lord. This is the kind of devotee I love most."

Truly, devotion is a way of life. One who is truly devoted is always immersed in the thoughts of the Lord. For him, everything is the Lord; everyone is a manifestation of the Lord; all work is God's work; nothing is yours and nothing is mine; everything belongs to Him and Him alone.

Baba tells us that devotion is that which enables the latent Divine Principle to manifest itself in the devotee's inner vision. Then, for the real devotee nothing exists other than God. To reach that stage, we must discharge our duties keeping God in mind constantly. Difficult though it is, this is the way prescribed...

22

Karma and Bhagya

"Utilise the capacity for action (karma) with which you are endowed to liberate yourself. The law of karma holds out hope for you; as the karma, so the consequence."

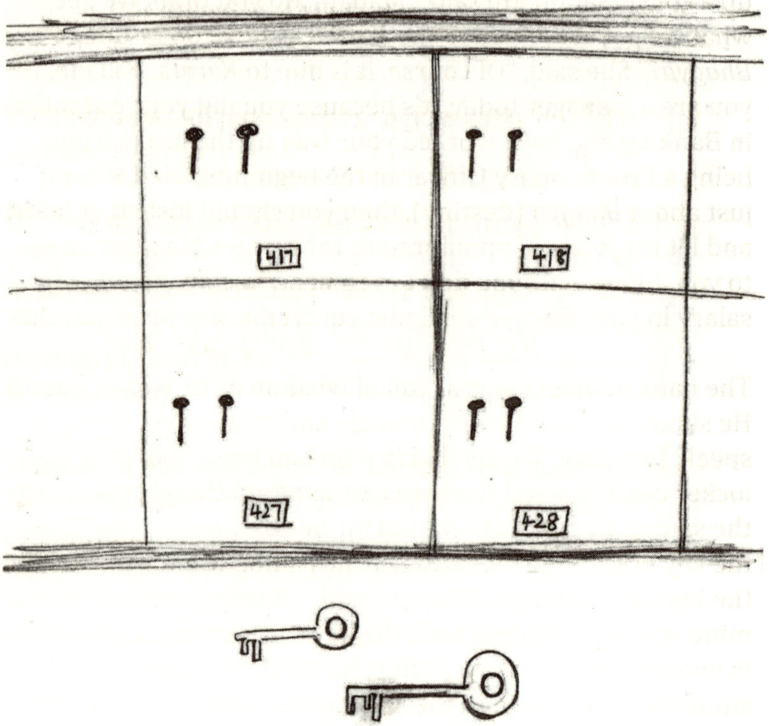
417
418
427
428

The bank manager was quite a gossip monger. He had tales to tell about everyone in the neighbourhood.

One day as *Bhagyashree* was waiting for her turn to operate her bank locker, she started flicking through the pages of a newspaper on the table. An article called *'Karmyogi'* caught her eye. The bank manager saw her reading it and picked up a conversation. He said, "Madam, do you think we get what we get in life due to the *Karma* that we do or due to our *Bhagya?*" She said, "Of course, it is due to *Karma*. Tell me, if you are a manager today, it's because you did your education in Banking and have worked your way up the ranks from being a Probationary Officer in the beginning. Had it been just about *Bhagya* (destiny), then you should just sit at home and let the letter of appointment for being a Manager come to you. Better still, you don't even need to come to work. The salary in your *Bhagya* shall just get credited to your account."

The bank manager was as full of wisdom as he was of gossip. He shook his head disapprovingly and cleared his throat to speak. Just then, the aged lady who had been operating her locker came out and the manager ushered Bhagyashree into the safe vault room. He waited for her to insert her key into the key hole of the locker, before inserting his master key in the key hole adjacent. Then he said, "Your key is your *karma*, mine is *bhagya*. Unless both the keys are operated, the locker is not going to open." So saying, he swiftly twisted the keys simultaneously, opened the safe, turned around on his heel and left the room.

Bhagyashree was stumped. Yes! Both the keys were equally important. Either one without the other was useless. Slowly she took out her gold bangles from the locker and slipped them onto her wrist. As she closed the safe, she realised that locking it could be done just by the *karma* key. She realised that *karma* was the present. Without it, even the *Bhagya* key alone wouldn't work. And only *karma* was in her control. *Bhagya* came into the picture only when *karma* was at work. If *karma* sat around doing nothing, what could *bhagya* do alone? It is as simple as saying, if you want to win a lottery, you have to at least buy a lottery ticket!

God gives us the opportunity to perform. He gives us the opportunity to do good *karma*. But *bhagya* is in His hands. Nothing happens unless He wills it to happen. But, at the same time, He too expects you to do your bit.

Don't let time just tick by. When you wake up, get up. When you get up, do something. Now whether you do good or bad is what decides what kind of future you are headed for.

23

A Divine Slumber

"Whatever services you render, do not feel that you are serving others, but you are serving God Himself. Even while serving food to your family or to a needy person, consider that God has come in that form and you are offering it to God Himself."

120/80
Jai Shree Ram!
Jai Shree Ram!
Jai Shree Ram!

The operation was soon to begin. Sanjay had been given a mild sedative before being wheeled into the operation theatre. He was made to lie down on the operation table, his arms stretched on either side on a cross. Huge overhead discs of lights were focussed on him.

The anaesthetist came close to his ear and whispered, "Sir, if you take any kind of drug or narcotic, please tell us. It will help us to take better care of you." Sanjay shook his head and said, "I don't take anything of that sort." The anaesthetist looked pleased as she pushed the cannula into the vein at his wrist.

She said, "Sir, please say the name of your chosen Lord and I shall repeat after you." Sanjay said, "Jai Shri Ram." She repeated after him, "Jai Shri Ram" once, twice, thrice... till Sanjay said, "Jai Shreeee Raaaam," and he zoned out. He was completely anaesthetised. The surgery was performed by the surgeon and his team. Everything was done and over. He had to be now brought out of anaesthesia. The doctors were waiting for him to 'wake up'. As the anaesthetist felt that he was 'coming back', she started reciting 'Jai Shri Ram, Jai Shri Ram..." In that inebriated condition, Sanjay mumbled softly, "Jai... Shreee... Raaam..."

Later, when he reflected on this and narrated it to his wife, a thought came to his mind, "What a beautiful way of going into and coming out of anaesthesia the doctor had devised." She was only doing her duty. It was her job to anaesthetise the patient. It was how she was conducting herself that made all the difference. Bhagwan Baba says, "Duty without love is deplorable duty with love is desirable; love without duty is divine."

Here is another anecdote... A very wealthy man could not sleep at night because he was always worried about his properties being damaged, burgled, money being stolen, bank being looted, etc.

So miserable was he with his sleeplessness that he sought help from an astrologer who told him to liquidate all his properties and convert them into a big block of gold. The man did just that and buried the gold brick into the ground. He would inspect it everyday to check if it was there. The gardener noticed this rather odd behaviour of the man and got to the bottom of the secret.

The first opportunity that came his way, the gardener took away the gold brick and absconded. The neighbour watched all the drama from her window. The following day the man came to check on his treasure and realised that the gold had been stolen. He cried bitterly.

Seeing him cry, the neighbour came in and said, "Oh! Why are you crying? Are you looking for your gold brick?" The man nodded in disbelief. She said, "I saw your gardener dig this up yesterday, and I snatched it from him and kept it with me. Here it is." Saying so, she handed a packet neatly wrapped in brown paper. It was meticulously taped and sealed. On it was written, 'The neighbour's gold brick'.

The man was so relieved. He hugged her and thanked her no end. He then took the gold brick inside and kept it in the darkest corner of his closet. A year later, he died peacefully. When his heirs opened that packet, it contained an ordinary brick; a building brick!

Why do you think the neighbour did what she did? She knew that the old man was never going to use that brick. He would never need to because he had enough to go by. All he needed was peace of mind. She succeeded in making him comfortable. Love without duty is truly Divine!

As they say, "Work is worship, duty is God." Everyone works. Everyone does something or the other. But, it is how we execute our duties that matters.

24

Stop This Hue and Cry

"What is this body? It is a perishable leather bag with nine holes but not like a resplendent diamond. No fragrance, but only foul smell emanates from it every moment. It is made up of flesh, bones and faecal matter. Should we develop attachment with this body?" — BABA

We have all heard about the *Bhagvad Purana* being told to King Parikshit in the seven days preceding his foretold time of death by snake bite. It is said that even after the sixth day of listening to Shukadeva's discourse, Parikshit was still scared of death and attached to his mortal frame.

Then Shukadeva told him a story. This is how it goes – A king once got lost in a forest while he was out hunting. Night fell and the sounds of wild animals growling and barking scared the wits out of him. He came across a shabby-looking hut from which emanated some light from a rusted old oil lamp. The man in the hut was incapacitated and could only crawl a little from here to there. The flesh of some dead animals hung from the ceiling which he had half eaten earlier. In a corner of the hut was a space which he had designated to answer the call of nature. The stench that emanated from the hut was so foul and obnoxious that the king could not breathe.

But, if he went out, he would surely fall prey to the carnivores of the jungle. So, he somehow brought himself to ask the man to allow him to spend the night in the hut that was nothing short of a hell-hole. The man said, "Whosoever I allow staying for a night refuses to go away in the morning. They create hue and cry, and they want to stay for longer. I cannot keep you here.

The king pleaded and, finally, the man agreed after repeating again very firmly that the king must leave, first thing in the morning.

Strangely, the smell emanating from the dead animals and human refuse had a terribly intoxicating effect on the king and he slept extremely well that night. It was well past dawn when the king was rudely woken up by the angry man, who ordered him to vacate his hut. The king was so well rested and relaxed that he forgot the purpose of his stay and begged the man to allow him to stay a few more nights. A heated exchange of words ensued. Both were adamant and argued and hurled abuses at each other.

Here Shukhadeva paused and asked, "Oh king Parikshit, do you think the king was being wise and prudent in begging to stay longer in the hut?"

Parikshit said, "Absolutely not! What a fool the king was to ask to stay in that hell hole full of stench and decay? How foolish of him to forget the purpose of his stay in the hut! Had it been for me, I would have run away at the first break of dawn. Who would want to sleep in a place that stinks of faecal matter, urine and the flesh of dead animals?"

Shukhadeva said softly, "Your majesty, that foolish king is you! The time allotted to you is getting over tomorrow. You have forgotten the purpose for which you were given this birth. You are intoxicated by this body that is nothing short of a hell hole. It is time for you to stop making such a ruckus and cut the ties that bind and proceed to the abode of the Lord, from where you have come."

With these words, Parikshit understood the meaning of life and, finally, started preparing for death.

One of the most valuable messages the scriptures convey is this: Carry on your legitimate duties, discharge your obligations, and live up to your rights; but do not allow attachment to grow. Be like a trustee so far as family, riches, reputation, knowledge and skills are concerned. Leave them gladly aside, when the call of death comes.

25

Be Like the Cow

"The headmaster knows that he is only the caretaker, not the owner. He is not attached to these articles; he knows that they belong to the government. So, too, feel that your family, house, property, car, etc. are all the Lord's property and you are just a trustee; be unattached and be ready to give them up without any murmur, at a moment's notice!"

MILK

A man had five children. They often asked him to give them a share of his huge property. But the old man said, "Nothing doing. I will write a Will. You will get everything after I die. Do you think I will take anything with me?

Everyone knows that no one can take anything along after death. Even the great King Alexander could take nothing along. I am just an ordinary man. Don't worry; you will all get your share."

The children were disgruntled. Many a times, they tried to persuade the father to reconsider, but the father was obstinate. He would not relent. Resultantly, the children were disrespectful and non-caring at times.

One day he visited a friend's farm. He saw a farm hand feeding fresh green fodder to the cows. Thereafter, he milked the cows and brought in a huge container of milk. On the other hand, he saw that a litter of pigs were scurrying around. They were basically eating waste from here and there. Not much was being fed to them. Only the leftovers from the kitchen that no one wanted to eat were given to the pigs.

The man asked his farmer friend to throw some light on the matter. He asked the farmer, "The cow is giving you milk, no doubt, so you feed it well and look after all its needs. But you don't bother about the pigs. Eventually, you will cut them up and get bacon and bam. You will probably even use their bristles. So, why don't you treat them well?"

The farmer said, "The cow gives a little of herself everyday. The pig shall be of value only after it dies. Who thinks of the future? We shall think of that when we come to it. Right now, I love my cows. I sell the milk and earn good money from them! So, I feed them well. See!"

The man went home deep in thought. He realised that he was being treated like a pig. Had he behaved like a cow, his children would have treated him like a cow. They would have respected him more.

The very next day he listed out whatever he wanted to give to his children and wrote out a Will. He gave access to the properties to the children so that they could enjoy the benefits. At the same time, the old man was shrewd enough to not pass on the ownership because he had read enough stories in the newspapers of aged parents being left high and dry after the children had milked them... and he was smart enough to tell his children that if they misbehaved, he would change the Will!

This reminds me of an old man who was dying. He gave away his property to his three sons. But, instead of dying, he became better. The sons turned the other way and refused to look after him. He was miserable. At the advice of a friend, he filled up an old chest with stones and locked it. He told his sons that he was going to Haridwar and taking the chest full of gold coins with him. Now the sons started lip service again. All three told him that he was old and infirm, so he should not go on such an arduous journey and they would look after him. Each tried to outdo the other. So, the father was made comfortable again. And he made the best of the put-on affection and respect. Eventually, the old man had to die one day, as we all do. The sons performed his last rites with grandeur. When they broke open the old chest ... well don't you think they deserved those stones?

Each person's circumstances in life are different. Prudence and common sense are the best fall backs!

26

Free To Do As I Please

"Limit your desires to your capacity and amongst them; choose those that grant lasting joy. Do not run after fashion and public approval and strain your resources. Stick to your own code of rules that regulate your life based on your spiritual progress."

There is a fable about the Emperor of China sending his people to invite a sage who lived in the Himalayas to become the Prime Minister of China. When the messengers reached there after a long journey, the sage was taking a dip in the river that ran by his hermitage. The messengers had to wait a while till he came out and did his prayers. After paying respects to him, the men very solemnly told the sage the purpose of their visit.

The sage patiently heard the proposition from the messengers. He smiled; a minute later, he laughed out loud and said, "Are you sure your Emperor wants me to become the Prime Minister?"

"Yes, the Emperor has heard of your wisdom from many. He sends his salutations and asked us to escort you respectfully to China to adorn the seat of the Prime Minister." The sage laughed till his eyes grew moist. The messengers looked at each other in discomfort. They didn't know what to make of this reaction.

After a while, the Hermit wiped the tears from his eyes and said, "I too have heard of the Emperor of China. Tell me, is there a Chapel in the palace that has a diamond-studded turtle embedded in the altar?" "Yes, yes that is right!" said one of them excitedly. He was happy that he had hit the right chord now. The sage's interest had been ignited. Great!

"And I believe that everyday, the Emperor and his clan pray and offer obeisance to that turtle." "Yes! That's true! You know everything! You are all in all!"

They were standing close to the river. The sage pointed to a turtle waddling happily in the muddy slush and said, "If I were to send this turtle to take up the place of that turtle, in the altar, do you think he would be happy?" The man replied, "I doubt sir ... I am not sure."

The sage said, "Even if I bathe and scrub it till it shines and make it wear a jacket studded with diamonds?" "I don't think so," said the messenger in a faltering voice.

The sage raised his voice and said with the courage of conviction, "You just think, he won't. But I know it for a fact! No one can be happy stuck in one position. Even if it is a position of honour! Go and tell your Emperor that for nothing would I give up the fresh air and water I revel in. The place I live in is heaven on Earth. For nothing would I give up my freedom of body, mind and spirit. I was born free and so shall I die! Here I am free to do as I please. I am my own master. There I shall have to bow to your Master. And I shall not do it!"

This reminds me of the great Philosopher Diogenes. He was dining one evening on lentils and bread when he was seen by one of the king's courtiers. The courtier said, "You shall not have to live on lentils if you learn subservience to the king." Diogenes smiled softly and said, "If you learn to live on lentils, you shall not have to be subservient to the king!"

27

Dog-Poop

"When you do not discriminate the process and purpose of every act, and go ahead doing them with no understanding, you reduce them to a funny fossilised routine."

The Chief Minister was expected to arrive any minute for a large program where hundreds of people had gathered.

There was an oil lamp in place at the corner of the stage for the ceremony of 'lighting of the lamp'. Some incense sticks had been lit to create a sweet smelling ambience. A large number of marigold garlands and rose bouquets were in place for welcoming the VIPs.

Just as the security head and all organisers had cleared everything and given the green signal of all 'OK', one of the sniffer dogs that was a part of the security cluster that checked the stage area for any kind of explosives, etc., cleared his bowels, just next to the red carpet area. Now this was a big problem as it was just a few feet away from where all the VIPs were to alight.

Just then the siren of the escort jeeps started blaring. That meant that some minister or super VIP was arriving. The in-charge saw the offensive smelling heap and panicked. There was no way to clean it up now. What to do? So in a split second he took two-three garlands of marigold flowers from the ones that they had in place to welcome the VIPs and placed them over the mound of poop. He quickly grabbed a pack of aggarbattis from the corner of the stage and stuck 7-8 aggarbattis over the flowers so that the stink emanating from the mound would not get noticed.

In less than a minute, a Minister arrived. He was welcomed with a garland. He saw the mound of flowers with the incense burning and thought it must be a sacred place. So he bowed, payed obeisance to the spot before taking his place on the Dias. The next VIP and the next and all that followed, did a repeat of what the first minister had done. Some of them even made offerings of money at the spot. One of them knelt down and bowed.

The in-charge who was watching all of the drama was keeping his fingers crossed. He almost choked when one of them bowed and touched his head on the flowers.

Finally, the Chief Minister came. By now the mound of flowers had become bigger. He alighted from the car and his gaze fell on the 'spot'. He didn't want to be labelled any less appropriate in social and religious etiquette. He knew that the media had all cameras on him. In a show of respect, he folded his hands and made a deep bow and offered prayers.

Well! The program commenced and the Chief Minister amongst other things thanked the organisers for providing him an opportunity to pay obeisance at this holy spot. Sometime later, the program was over. Everyone dispersed. The in-charge and his team cleared up the premises and shovelled away the 'holy mound' complete with flowers, into the garbage truck.

Besides the laugh... do think about this... Sometimes there are ancient beliefs that have no meaning. Incidents such as the one told above do make us realise that we need to use our heads too. Let us understand the 'whys' of things. Let us not be blind followers.

Let us clarify here that we firmly believe that most of our Hindu rituals have a reason behind them. Our culture is based on a deep understanding of spirituality and science. So, if we really delve into it, there is a wealth of knowledge therein. Since people don't have the time or the inclination to know for themselves, many a time they get fooled by palmists, astrologers, soothsayers and the like.

28

The Winning Toss

"Above all, realisation depends on Jnanashakti or the force and clarity of wisdom, the self-confidence that flows from the mastery of the situation. This is a gift of grace from God."

A group of children were representing the school in a festival of music. Group entries in various categories had been invited and many teams from four states were participating.

One of the teams was being led by its music teacher called Zubini. She knew that the team was very talented and had practised very hard. The auditions started. With their hearts in their mouths, they cleared round one and were one of the ten teams shortlisted from a total of twenty-seven.

The second round was tougher. There was an amazing display of talent. It was a joy to see the shining faces of the participating children. There was so much enthusiasm and energy all over. With hearts pounding and limbs trembling, Zubini's team performed. This performance brought them to stand as one of three. The next and final round would be held on the next day.

The team leader made them practise in the late evening too. At the same time, she was careful not to overtire them, for freshness was an important thing that factored in musical performances. She realised that her team was really good and had a fair chance to win. But somewhere she felt that the children were lacking confidence. Their body language was lacking buoyancy and poise.

The teacher was worried. That night passed. In the morning, she told them that before the competition, they would all pray in the little temple in the premises. So, they all prayed fervently. Each child prayed for success. The teacher prayed for confidence.

Once the prayer was over, she took out a coin from her purse and said, "I am going to flip this. If it's heads, we win. If it's tails, they lose." She flipped the coin. Heads it was. "Yayyy!" The children shouted out in glee. "Shhh," she said, "Now this is a secret between God and us. We are going to win! Give it your best; and do it with a smile ... Come back with the trophy!"

They performed. A scintillating performance they put up! Their faces beamed; their faces exuded confidence. They made it to number one, without a doubt!

Later, while they were celebrating with the teacher, one of them said, “Ma’am your coin flip came true! That was wonderful!” She said, “My dears! Just go over what I said, ‘Heads we win; Tails they lose!’ Had I flipped ‘tails’, they would still have lost; we would still have won! It was a win-win situation for us all the way! Confidence is the deciding factor when the race is amongst equals!”

Teachers are as important as parents in grooming a child. A bad teacher admonishes and complains. A good teacher teaches and explains. The best teacher encourages and applauds!

29

The Best Tea

"Be simple in your method of living, have saatwik (pure) food and moderate recreation."

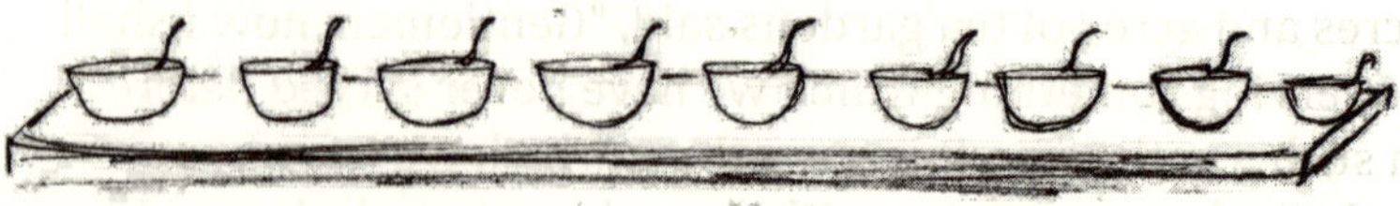

A group of elderly gentlemen were at a tea-sampling meet. The choicest varieties of tea were being served in small portions. Most of the teas were of exotic flavours and very expensive.

The distinguished-looking gentlemen wore designer suits, tuxedos or *kurtas*. Most of them were platinum blondes. Their expensive spectacles oozed class. Their clothes were ironed such that the creases could draw blood. Their shoes shone such that you could use them in place of a mirror, to groom that unruly strand of hair tickling your face! Some of them spoke heavily accented English, while others chose to speak in chaste Hindi.

One thing was common amongst them. They all had style! They were a class apart!

The afternoon moved at snail's pace as several rounds of tea were served at leisure. There were no hurries and no worries! Some teas were served green, some black, others with milk and sweeteners. Some were flavoured with cinnamon; cardamom; ginger and other exotic ones with raspberry and blueberry too.

There was an array of sweeteners too ... one could choose from brown demerara, white sugar, stevia, honey, artificial sweeteners and good old molasses too! The small eats had dry fruits, sweets and savouries of every kind one could think of. To make it short, one was spoilt for choice ...

Towards the end of the tea-tasting session, and after many rounds of applause, the organiser of the meet who owned acres and acres of tea gardens said, "Gentlemen, now I shall be serving something which we have never served before in such a gathering. It is something which we have kept exclusively for ourselves. After much contemplation and debate, we have decided to share the flavour that we have held close to our hearts for decades. Please enjoy."

In the finest of porcelain cups was served small quantities of tea brewed with milk and sugar. Everyone drank it to the last drop. It tasted like ambrosia!"

The host waited till everyone had finished bottoms up. He then said, "Did you like it my friends?" There was intense clapping from all. He said, "This is what we serve to our farm hands. This is the cup of tea I enjoy most in the company of my workers!"

Truly it's the simplest things in life that are the best. They generally don't cost much. And they are easy to get too.

Think about this –

Despite so many colours — black and white are the classiest.

Despite so many cosmetics — a smile is all you need to look good.

Despite so many tourist spots — the best place to relax is at home.

Despite so many fancy fabrics — nothing beats cotton.

Despite so many drinks available — water is still the best to quench thirst.

Despite so much talks about fashion — simplicity is most appealing.

Despite so much to surf on the Internet — surfing the inner net is most soothing!

30

Drunken Businessman

"Neethi means right conduct. It implies right behaviour in harmony with the conditions of the particular time, place and society."

A very rich business tycoon had a whole lot of people working in his industry. He had a small township where all his employees used to live. The businessman was a very upright man with a high moral character. He was usually very respectful towards all, especially women.

One night he got drunk. He started walking on the streets of the township in that inebriated condition. He passed some lewd comments on a young girl who was walking on the street. No one dared to say anything to him.

When he started abusing and using offensive language to all who came his way, the old family cook happened to notice him. He caught hold of him and physically dragged him home.

In the morning, everyone was sure that the cook, who was an old man, would surely lose his job. The businessman had a faint recollection of the night's happenings. He asked his secretary to explain to him what had happened last night. The Secretary narrated all, but added some spice to the narrative. Perhaps he had a score to settle with the old cook.

The boss remained silent for a while. He then called the cook and said, "Thank you for saving me from further embarrassment. I don't remember exactly what happened last night. But had it not been for you, perhaps I would have indulged in something I would have to be ashamed of today.

There is an old couplet by Saint Kabir:

"Nindak niyare rakhiye, Aangan kuti chavaye.

Bin paani sabun bina, Nirmal kare suhaye."

(Keep a critic in your house; he will cleanse your temperament without soap or water!)

As a child, I remember reading a story of a little girl named Patty, who was in the habit of telling lies. Her father often told her that lying was a sin, but the habit was deep-rooted and, hence, difficult to break.

One day Patty was playing with her baby brother. The infant fell down and grazed his knees. Father asked her if she had pushed him. She said, "No Papa, I didn't." Father did not believe her. While tending to the toddler's wounds, he rebuked her.

Patty was infuriated that she had been unfairly reprimanded. When father was engrossed in reading the newspaper, she deliberately pushed the baby. He fell and cried bitterly. Father yelled, "Patty, did you push him over?" "No Papa," she said rebelliously. Father asked in a stern voice, "Telling lies?" "No Papa," she said defiantly.

That evening Papa took Patty aside and asked her to show him her tongue. As she stuck her tongue out, he swiftly gave her a little cut downwards on the tongue with a knife. She yelped in pain. Then he said, "Patty, this is a little punishment to you for all the lies you have been telling. Now, every time you speak, this is going to hurt you. Let the hurt be a reminder to you of what is going to happen if you lie again. If you give me another chance, I shall use my scissors to snip off a bit off your tongue!"

In today's times of so much being talked about children's rights, etc., this may amount to child abuse. I read this story in my childhood (more than 40 years back), when the good old maxim of 'Spare the rod and spoil the child' was the golden rule of disciplining children. In this case, perhaps, the father was a little too harsh...

But, the story still has a very strong message. Parents have to discipline their children while they are small. Sometimes I think that it is lack of discipline in the home that has led to our society being what it is today.

31

Punishment for Birbal

"You must go through the vicissitudes of life with forbearance and become attractive jewels. You should not allow yourselves to be overwhelmed by difficulties. Develop self-confidence and have firm faith in God."

There are numerous tales where Birbal was consulted for helping the Emperor Akbar to decide difficult cases so that justice could be done. Birbal was considered to be the wisest man in the kingdom. Due to this, he earned the respect of many and the jealousy of some too.

Once Birbal committed an error. It was documented that Birbal had made a mistake. So, as per the law of the land, he had to be punished. Emperor Akbar was pained to see Birbal standing in court as an 'accused' waiting for punishment to be pronounced. In his heart of hearts, Akbar wanted to pardon Birbal for he felt that for the so many times that Birbal had brought honour to the kingdom and its people, one small error should be pardoned. But, the Ministers who were jealous of Birbal were waiting to hear the punishment, like hawks waiting for their prey.

Akbar's throat went dry. With great difficulty, he started to speak, hoping that Birbal would find a way out of this mess. In a choked voice, he said, "Birbal, no one is above the law. You have made a mistake, so you will have to be punished. But, for all your service to me, I give you the right to choose the person who shall decide your punishment. After that, you shall have to honour it."

Birbal looked around. The senior ministers looked up expectantly thinking that Birbal would trust them to do justice. After thinking for a few minutes, Birbal said, "Can you call the gardener? I would be happy to have him decide my punishment." There was a suppressed laughter in Akbar's court. What did the gardener know? And how stupid of Birbal to submit to his whims!

Well, the gardener was called and told of Birbal's wish. He was so overwhelmed with the thought of having been given such a huge responsibility that he said, "I cannot decide this alone. Let me consult my fellow gardeners. Give me at least two days to decide."

Eventually, he asked for more time and after a week, the entire gardener community of the city filed into Akbar's court. Most of them were in tears. The gardener said, "Birbal! Oh Birbal! You are very dear to us. Don't take this personally. We all have to abide by the law. We have been discussing this matter for a week. We have spent sleepless nights mulling over the problem. With great difficulty, we have decided that, we have decided that... please forgive us Birbalji! We hold you in very high esteem, but this is a *dharam-sankat* for us. We have decided that you must ... that you must ... you must pay five hundred gold pieces!!!" The gardener broke down and wept profusely.

Birbal smiled. Akbar heaved a huge sigh of relief. Just five hundred gold coins! That was no big deal for a person of Birbal's stature. Birbal had done it again! He knew that each person can think only up to his perspective or restricted viewpoint and not beyond. For a gardener, who was a simpleton, who spent his day looking after the flowers and the trees, money was not something he would think about too much. For someone who lived so close to nature, and found contentment in the simple things of life, for someone who perhaps seldom thought about money and its worth, for someone whose needs were limited, five hundred gold coins was a humongous amount of wealth. But, for Birbal, it was a pittance!

The presence of mind of Birbal had done it again!

32

Stuck in the Muck

"Through the process of 'giving up', great things can be achieved. Cultivate detachment, and the Lord will attach Himself to you. The past is beyond recovery; those days are gone. But tomorrow is coming towards you. Resolve to sanctify it with Love, Service and Sadhana."

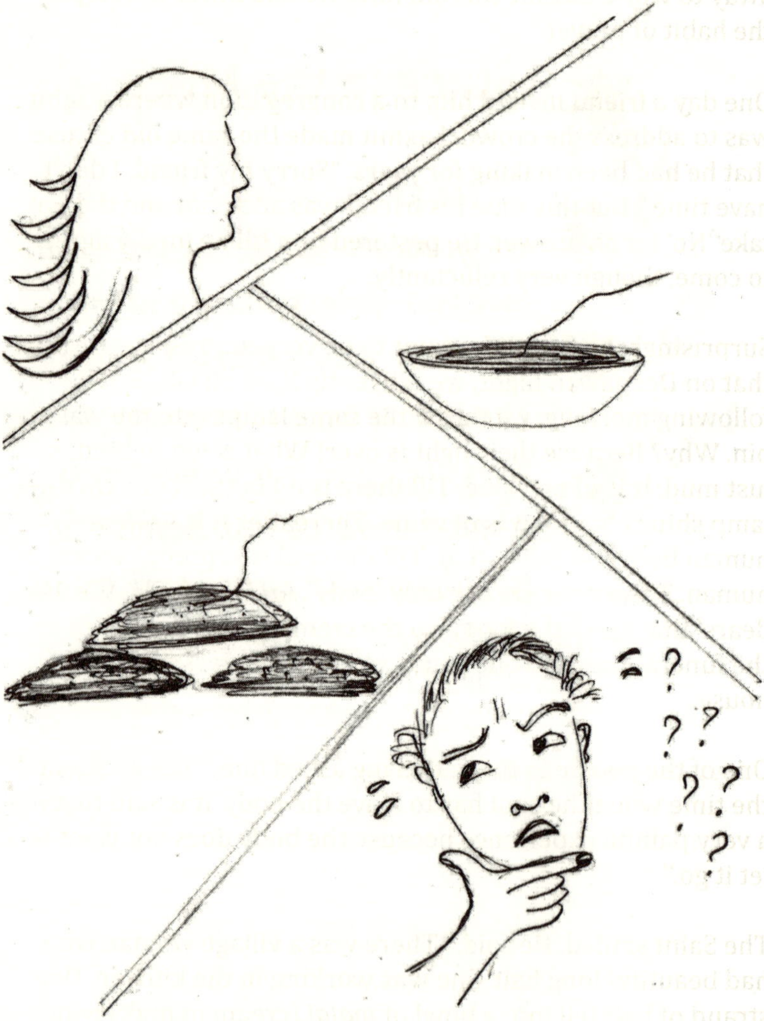

Laxmit was verily a typical family man. His life revolved around his home and office. Like clockwork, he would attend office from 9 am to 5 pm. He would come straight home and spend time with his parents, wife and children. Such was his routine for years and years. The children grew up and went away to work. Laxmit was old now. He had never developed the habit of prayer.

One day a friend invited him to a congregation where a Saint was to address the crowd. Laxmit made the same old excuse that he had been making for years, "Sorry my friend, I don't have time." But this time his friend was adamant and did not take 'No' for an answer. He pestered him till he finally agreed to come, though very reluctantly.

Surprisingly he found the saint to be very impressive. He said that on Deepawali night, we diligently light oil lamps. The following morning, we throw the same lamps into the waste bin. Why? Because their light is over! What is left behind is just mud. It is of no value. Till there is oil in the lamp, till the lamp shines bright, it is of value. Thereafter it is useless. The human body too is like that. Till the soul is present, we are human. Thereafter, we are only 'body'. And it's the 'nears and dears' that carry the 'body' to the crematorium and perform the funeral rites. No one wants to keep a lifeless body in the house.

One of the people in the gathering asked him, "Tell us about the time when the soul has to leave the body. It is said that it's a very painful experience because the body does not want to let it go."

The Saint smiled. He said, "There was a village woman who had beautiful long hair. She was working in the kitchen. One strand of hair fell into a bowl of *malai* (cream of milk) lying on the kitchen shelf.

Later, while she was clearing the cowshed of cow dung and making cow dung cakes, a few strands of hair fell into the dung while she did this.

The following day when she was putting away the dried cow dung cakes, she noticed a stray strand of hair sticking out of it. Inadvertently she tried to pull it out. It was stuck in the muck. She tugged at it a bit harder. It broke but it didn't come out fully. After her evening chores in the kitchen, she was setting aside the bowl of *malai* and noticed a strand of hair in it. She plucked it out and cast it away. That transition was smooth as silk."

The Saint concluded his discourse. Everyone dispersed. Laxmit could not sleep all night. He was seventy-five now. Sooner or later, it would be time to leave the world. What would it be like when his soul had to leave the body? Would it be stuck in the muck, like the hair in the dung? Or would it slip out smooth as silk, like the hair in the *malai?* Stuck or smooth? Smooth? Stuck? Muck? Oh my God! What a mess I am in! I have never turned Godwards. Time to wake up!

Well, it's never too soon or too late to wake up...

The time is 'now' for each one of us. Connecting with God is a legacy that is our privilege as well as our duty.

Baba tells us that we should not wait till old age to take to the path of spirituality. If we start early and drive slowly, then we shall reach safely. We should practise detachment from now on; practise it little by little, for a day will come sooner or later when we will have to give up all that we hold dear.

33

A Very Good Maid

"It is the noble thoughts of the mother which make the children great."

Yackety
Yak!
Yak! Yak!

Down the memory lane, I remember an auntie who would often walk into our home (my parental home), at odd hours of the day. Her husband was in the merchant navy, so she was usually by herself. Her twin boys, then of the age of eight or nine, were a naughty twosome. They were known for playing cricket in the park adjacent and breaking the window panes of the houses adjoining. They would abuse loudly the servants and maids in the house, which were aplenty. Their grades at school are best left to rest in peace. The teachers had a charter of complaints about them!

The afternoon was the time when we would all sit around in Mama's room, doing our homework or colouring or just playing the fool. Whether it was reading or writing, Maths or Science, English or Hindi, our mother would take keen interest in everything we did and it was just reassuring to have her around. She was our 'go-to-person' for everything and we just took it for granted that because she was Mama, so she was always there.

One such afternoon, auntie walked in. My mom was a little hassled to see auntie, for this would encroach upon our homework time. I remember my mother asking her, "Aren't your children home at this time? Don't you supervise their homework?" She said, "Yes but their music instructor is over. Besides, I have a very good maid. And in case they need anything, the driver is always in waiting."

Over the years, I remember my mother's irritated face whenever the lady would walk in and rant about how naughty her boys were. Every anecdote was punctuated by, "But I have a very good maid. And in case of any problem, the driver is always in waiting." It seems we heard this a hundred times over.

In our home, where my mother would cook, wash, iron, teach and do everything possible under the Sun, there was no sign of a maid. We as innocent kids thought a maid was a 'high and mighty lady', who had the controlling prowess of an army major. In my childish mind's eye, a maid was a large, burly woman who was in control of everything. She could put those brats across her knees and spank the daylights out of them!

Well, that was four-odd decades ago.

Driving past that auntie's house one day, I happened to spot her in a wheel-chair. A lady attendant was wheeling her slowly. I stopped by to say 'Hello!' to her. Her son was sitting in the garden under a gazebo, drinking beer, while the maid slowly wheeled the old lady up and down in the driveway.

Seeing me talking to auntie, the son walked up to me. We exchanged pleasantries. He told me that he was settled in Boston while his twin brother was in Leicester. Their father was no more. I said, "Oh! I'm so sorry to hear about uncle." He said, "My brother and I visit here twice in a year. We talk to Ma over the weekend. During the week, there is really no time. You know how busy life is abroad. All day there is no time to call."

I said, "Oh! So, auntie lives here alone?" "No, no," he said emphatically, "We have a very good maid. And in case of any problem, the driver is always in waiting."

"Yes, I'm sure," I murmured, trying to forge a smile. My step was a little unsteady as I took leave. Truly, life does come around full circle.

34

Travel Partners

"We must try to make the best of our present age, and try to do good and live happily. Past is past, it will never come again, and we are not sure of the future."

Three friends were on a business trip. After days of travel, they are tired. On the last night of their travel, they realised that they had only one *chapatti* left amongst the three of them. They could not make up their minds how to divide it or who should have it. So, they decided that all three of them would go to bed hungry. Whosoever had the best dream would get the *chapatti* as a reward in the morning.

So, all of them went to bed hungry. In the morning, they sat together to narrate their dreams. They kept the *chapatti* box in the middle. The first man said, "I dreamt that in my past birth, I was an Emperor. I had a huge empire and a huge army. I had many beautiful queens and many strong sons and beautiful daughters. I had hundreds of servants and maids to do my bidding. I was a great man. The world hailed me as the greatest Emperor of all times."

The second man said, "Hang on my friend. Wait till I tell you what my dream was. You shall be left wanting for what to say. I dreamt that three days from now, I shall become a very rich man. I shall have many factories. I shall have a huge bungalow in the poshest area of Delhi. I shall be doing business with a foreign collaboration. I shall have ten cars and a battalion of servants. Just wait till three days, I shall be a great man."

The third man was listening silently. After a few minutes, the first two looked at him questioningly. He said, "My friends, you are indeed great men. One of you was a great man and the other shall be a great man. I am honoured to know you. I am but a simpleton. You know I am a devotee of Lord Hanuman. Before sleeping, I prayed to Him to help us solve the problem. Hanumanji came in my dream and said, 'How can I allow my Bhakta to sleep on a hungry stomach? Get up and have the *roti*!' So, I got up in the middle of the night and ate the *roti*. I could not have possibly disobeyed my Lord. Could I?"

The other two looked at the box lying in the middle and realised what fools they had been.

In life too, there are all kinds of people. Some live in the past, like the first man. They dwell on past memories and glories. They lament the lost grandeur of the past and crib about the present always.

Others live constantly in the future like the second man. They are great at building castles in the air. They sit around and do nothing but dream and gossip.

The third are the kind that live in the present. They believe in doing things and having control over their thoughts, words and deeds! Which kind are you? Do think about it!

Dreams are but dreams. Whether we dream while asleep or we day-dream, a dream is a dream! It is better to live in the present. Everything is here and now. Past is past, it cannot come back. Future is unseen and uncertain. Live in the present and make it happy, the future shall automatically become good.

Make sure that you enjoy the journey; the destination is of secondary importance. Live in the moment. The future may or may not ... come. Life is uncertain. The difference between life and death is just one little breath!

35

Ground Allotment

"Forms of worship, or the phraseology of adoration, or the style of address may vary, but all religions are directed towards the same consummation. The same bloodstream circulates in all the limbs of the body. This is spoken of as the realisation of the Fatherhood of God and the Brotherhood of Man."

There was a large open ground in the middle of a town. The land belonged to the government. Because of paucity of funds, it was not being looked after and had become a dumping ground for garbage and refuse. Wild grasses were growing there. It was infested with snakes, rats, cockroaches, mosquitoes and the like. The village elders decided that something must be done about this breeding ground for vermin and disease.

There were various communities in the village, and people were very conscious of their groups and leanings. Each community was claiming that the land be allotted to them. As is common in such cases, everyone was outdoing the other in preparing their case as a claimant. After much discussion and argument from many quarters, they were still not able to decide what to do with the land.

So, eventually, it was proposed to let the various groups get the rights to use the land turn by turn for a week each. By draw of lots, the first week came to the Krishna devotees. They cleaned up the entire place. They organised religious discourses on the Geeta and the *Bhagwad Puran*. They sang *Krishna Bhajans* and danced together in celebration. But, only the Krishna devotees came for the celebrations. All others stayed away.

The following week the draw favoured the Christians. They sang carols and staged skits portraying the birth and life of Jesus. This time only the Christians were in attendance. The others abstained from participating.

The third week was allotted to the Durga Mata devotees. They organised *jagrans* all night where they sang devotional songs in praise of the Goddess Divine. They organised *langars* where they fed little prepubescent girls as *Kanyas*, as the living form of the Goddess. They gave bangles and *bindis* to the little girls too.

When all the groups had had their turns, it was time for a discussion. The seniors of the town were to decide who had done the best job and, hence, should be allotted the land for future use. The discussion grew intense and fiery. Everyone was a claimant.

One of the elders happened to look out of the window of the meeting room overlooking the ground. He saw that all the village children had gathered there. They were playing cricket. Some were playing; the others were cheering. What caught his eye was that children from the families of all religious groups were there. No one had kept away from the game. He kept watching for a few minutes. Then he said, "Friends, I request you all to come and watch the cricket match from this window." All of them watched for a few minutes. Each of them spotted his or her children or grandchildren there.

Then the old man said, "So, who should we allot the land to?" Everyone looked at each other and smiled. Yes!!! The land should be reserved for the children! Eventually, it was developed as a playground for children. All the groups took weekly turns in the cleaning and upkeep of the ground. What belonged to no one, now belonged to everyone!

Why should religion create barriers? God is one. He can be remembered and worshipped in many ways. But, God is one only. We can call Him by different names; we can reach Him by different paths, but He is one... only one.

Children have pure hearts. They know nothing about groups and barriers. Perhaps we too need to learn a thing or two from them. The Indians believe that the world is one family... *Vasudhaiva Kutumbakam!* We believe in the Fatherhood of God and the brotherhood of man!

36

Smart Move

"One has to be alert, vigilant and fully trained to meet all emergencies."

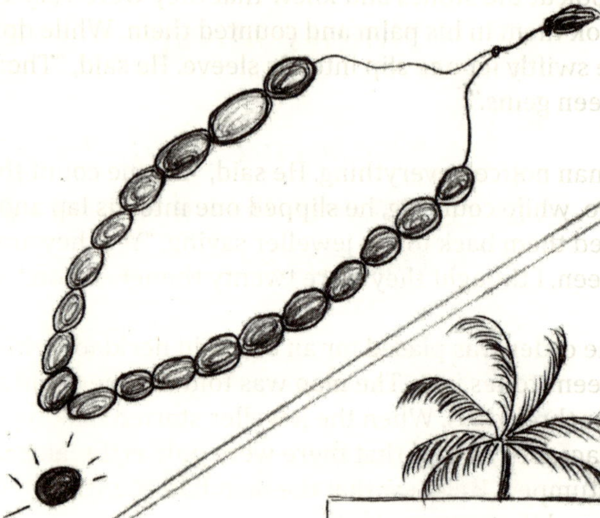

STRAWBERRY
MANIA
1. Useless Ambience
2. Exorbitant rates
3. Untidy and messy
Come in at our own risk

Grandfather had just died a few days back. The grandchildren were to be given the family jewels. Each one's share was earmarked to perfection. One of the grandsons was handed over a pouch of twenty green emeralds that was assigned to his name. The man took the emeralds to a jeweller and asked him to make him a necklace for his wife. The jeweller took one look at the stones and knew that they were very valuable. He took them in his palm and counted them. While doing so, he swiftly let one slip into his sleeve. He said, "There are nineteen gems."

The man noticed everything. He said, "Let me count them too. So, while counting, he slipped one into his lap and handed them back to the jeweller saying, "Yes they are indeed nineteen. I thought they were twenty though, I wonder..."

So, the order was placed for an emerald necklace with nineteen stones in it. The man was told that he could collect it after three days. When the jeweller started making the necklace, he realised that there were only eighteen stones. He was stumped. He knew that the man had counted them right there and there were nineteen.

So, what was the solution? Yes! The jeweller had to put in the first stone that he had so cleverly swindled; there was no alternative!

Sometimes you have to take the bull by the horns! Sometimes you have to answer in the same language as the one the other understands. Presence of mind and common sense are life skills that we must all develop. While it is wrong to wrong somebody, and it is equally wrong to sit quiet, if someone wrongs you. Don't let the world make a fool of you!

Here is another anecdote that is also about a smart move. Read on...

A highway restaurant in Goa was called 'The Coconut Retreat.' It had been there for many years, but business was meagre and as the years passed, it was declining steadily. The owner was affable; the ambience was cordial; the coconut plantation was neat, clean and healthy; the prices were reasonable, but business just wouldn't pick up.

The dejected owner made a drastic change just as a fluke. He changed the name to 'AINAM YRREBWARTS' and put up a board outside that said –

1. Useless ambience

2. Exorbitant rates

3. Untidy and messy

Come in at your own risk!

Every customer, especially youngsters, want to experiment with the unconventional. All of them stared at the board, smiled, giggled and said, "Let's try this... It looks different!" The owner just added a strawberry drink as a free welcome drink and business picked up. Soon the place was abuzz.

A little innovation goes a long way. Presence of mind and quick action is the key. Making the right move at the right time is what matters. If we are not able to react quickly to situations such-like, we shall miss the bus.

37

Daanveer Karan

"The most direct method of spiritual success is Nishkama karma (desireless action) — action without any attention or attachment to the fruit therefrom, action as duty, action as dedication, and action as worship."

Krishna's favourite disciple Arjuna was pestering Him to tell him why Karan was said to be the most charitable of them all.

Krishna pointed towards two mountains and they turned into gold. He said, "Arjuna, I give these to you. You, in turn, must donate them to the villagers in this area. See that you donate all of the bulk. Don't save any for yourself."

The next day, Arjuna gathered all the villagers together and proclaimed that he was going to give away portions of these mountains to them all, so they must all queue up. From morning, till sundown, Arjuna shovelled away, mounds of gold to the villagers. Strangely, the mountains seemed to not get diminished in size. Arjuna was baffled. He said, "Krishna, I am tired. I need a break. I will distribute the rest tomorrow." So, the same exercise went on the next day and the day after and the day-day-after. But the mountains were still the same size. Eventually, Arjuna had to give up.

Then Krishna called Karan and said, "Karan, these mountains are yours. Distribute them amongst the villagers." Karan called the villagers and bowed before them and said, "Brothers, please distribute these mountains amongst yourselves." Having said so, Karan walked away. He did not as much as look back to see what or how the villagers were doing.

Krishna smiled knowingly and said, "Arjun, you were behaving as if everything belonged to you and you were the donor. You were calculating the value of each portion of gold in your mind as you were giving it away. This is the difference between Karan and you. Look at him, he is totally detached. He just passed it on from me to them. He did not bat an eyelid or think twice! Now do you understand why they call him *Daanveer* Karan?"

On the flip side, let us tell you about a man who was known to be a miser. He had never given anything to anyone all his life. One day he went to the river to bathe. Suddenly, he felt he was drowning. He cried out for help. A man ran forward and stretched out his arm saying, "Here! Give me your hand." The drowning man kept screaming but wouldn't reach out for the hand outstretched.

Another young boy shouted, "Hey! Give me your hand!" But the drowning man, while gasping for breath and trying frantically to keep himself afloat, did not reach out for the hand extended.

One onlooker knew that the fellow was a miser; someone who had never given anything to anyone, even in his dream. He went closer saying, "My friend! Here, take my hand, come on..." In an instant, the fellow grabbed the hand and soon was out of the water.

What is the difference? The earlier two men had said, "Give me your hand..." For a man who has never ever given anything to anyone, even giving a hand was something he was unable to bring himself to do. When he heard, "Take my hand..." He did it immediately. The difference is in psyche.

There is great joy in giving. If God is kind to us and we have enough or surplus, it is important that we give too. Input-output are both important in life. Earning alone is not enough. We must share with those who don't have enough.

As humans, we eat and drink. Then we digest and remove the wastes from the body. If we only eat, eat and eat and do not expel the waste, what will happen? Exactly!

As we inhale and exhale, so too we must keep the inflow and outflow of wealth and good thoughts and deeds, an ongoing process. Even a river remains clean because it is always flowing. A pond where the water is stagnant starts to stink.

38

Dividing the *Roti* Again

"Develop your wisdom, not your egoism."

There is an old folktale about two cats that found a *roti* and asked a monkey to help them divide it into two equal halves. (See Sunrays for Wednesday). In that story, while trying to equalise the two portions of the *roti,* the monkey kept taking little bites from each of the two *roti* portions. Eventually, he ate up the entire *roti* and the two cats were left gaping! He succeeded in fooling the cats!

So, it seems that the monkey told the story of his ingenuity to his descendants to glorify how he had outsmarted the two cats of their *roti*. Oh! How we love to gloat over our cleverness!

But do you think the cats would not have told their children and grandchildren about their idiocy? And is it not prudent that we learn from our mistakes?

So, presently, the grandchildren of the monkey and the cats are the characters in our story. So, a pair of twin cats found a *roti* lying somewhere and decided to divide it equally. So, how should they divide it? A monkey saw them lurking around waiting to be invited in, as his grandfather had narrated.

But the cats were wiser now. So, the elder cat told the younger one that they should steer clear away of the cunning monkey, who was waiting for the *roti* to be put up for grabs.

The elder cat said that he would divide the *roti* very carefully and try his best that it is done equally. So, he tore the *roti* into two parts. Closing one eye to get a sharper view, he looked at it judgementally and said, "I think the two are equal." The younger one looked quite satisfied too. The elder cat said, "Since I have divided it, in all fairness you can take a pick of the two. Whichever one is left shall be mine." The younger cat happily took his share, hugged his elder brother and the matter was settled much to the disillusionment of the monkey who stood by watching the entire scene. He felt cheated!

Stories are stories, but let us not undermine their power to teach and leave deep and everlasting impressions on our minds.

Let me share with you that our father (Sh B.D. Tandon) is the youngest of three brothers. He remembers a time when the family jewels were to be divided amongst the ladies of the house. The eldest brother divided everything as per weight, using a jewellers weighing scale. He then told the youngest to take the first pick and himself took the last portion!

If the intention is to be fair and just, there is always a solution forthcoming. Mutual trust between members of the family is invaluable. There are differences in most families, but family matters are best settled behind closed doors and within the family. The litigation process in our country is slow and painful. There is a folk saying that after the litigation process is over... *"Jo jeeta, wo haarae jaisa; jo haara, wo moyae jaisa!"* Meaning that after the process of litigation is over ... the one who has won is as good (or as bad) as lost; and the one that has lost, is as good as dead!

39

The King's Shoe

"You must surrender your judgement to the Lord, and then Lord will assume full responsibility."

The King's Shoe

A king was once roaming the streets of the city as part of an annual religious procession. He saw that some people looked happy while others looked tense and forlorn.

The king walked on and an attendant walked behind him holding a large umbrella over his head to shield him from the scorching heat of the sun. The king suddenly felt that one of his feet was getting burnt as the heat from the ground permeated through the sole of his embroidered shoe. But why was just one of his feet feeling so? On examining, it was found that the sole of one of the shoes had fallen off few yards back and so the foot was feeling the intense heat.

The king's attendants quickly seated him on the side of the road and looked around for a cobbler. The cobbler was told to repair the king's shoe speedily. The cobbler stitched up the sole in a few minutes and the shoe was given back to the king.

The cobbler was asked how much his payment was. He said, "Nothing Sir, it is an honour for me that I could serve the king."

But the king insisted that the payment should be made. So, the cobbler was asked again how much he would charge. The cobbler was too embarrassed to ask for a few paise for the job. So, he said, "Well, give me whatever you deem fit. I shall accept it."

The attendant conveyed this to the king. The king casually said, "Then give him two villages!" And so it was!

And so is it with God too! We keep asking Him for petty things; tinsel and trash; and He keeps obliging us to make us happy, if only we would realise that He is the master of the entire universe. He can give us anything. Anything at all! All we need is to surrender to His will. Let Him decide. Let Him plan what is good for us.

My late father Justice Punchhi once wrote.

"Do not plan for God,

God has plans for you.

Life is an opportunity, avail it,

Leave it to Him to unfold your future.

You came to this world at His command,

You will vacate it at His behest.

Enjoy the rhythm of pain and pleasure set by Him,

Let Him regulate it.

You go on fighting the battle of life."

Swami says, "Total surrender, leaving everything to His Will is the highest form of devotion."

40

Row, Row, Row Your Boat

"The spiritual path is the path of detachment, of sense control, of rigorous mind training."

Chaubeyji wanted to cross the river one dark and windy night. He had come to the other side of the river to meet someone this morning. The day had just passed loitering around the festive bazaars and chit-chatting with old friends. In the company of his friends, he had a drink or two. As the day drew to a close, he realised that it was high time he went home to the other side of the river.

When he looked for a boatman, he found that there was no one around. Perhaps it really was very late. He looked around desperately and saw a small little boat near the river bank. He got into it and decided to row himself to the other side.

All night he kept rowing. It was difficult for him to keep awake because he was so tired after the day's activities. The wind blew harshly and it was quite a task for Chaubeyji to keep himself awake as well as afloat in the water.

His biceps hurt as he continued to row. He strained his eyes to see the other side of the shore but the moonlight was too dim for the new moon was barely a sickle in the dark sky.

He stared at the crescent in the sky and wondered when the solar deity would wake up. After what seemed like eternity, the glow of dawn lit up the dark waters.

But, what was this? Was he still on this side of the shore? But he had rowed hard all night. He had not rested even for a second. How could it be so?

His tired eyes narrowed slowly on to a rope. And he realised that the boat was tied to the shore by the rope. He had rowed all night, but because of the rope, he had gotten nowhere. All his hard work had resulted into nothing.

How stupid of him to not untether the boat before getting into it! He was just where he was last night ...

So too it is in life. Sometimes, we are so attached to the mundane that all efforts on the spiritual path are exercises in futility.

If we want to reach the other side of the *Bhavsagar*, we have to cut the ties that bind.

This story reminded me of a poem that I learnt in nursery school. This is how it was – 'Row, row, row your boat, gently down the stream. Merrily, merrily, merrily, merrily, life is but a dream!'

It's alright for a child to feel that life is but a dream, but as adults, we do need to realise that the dream is going to end one day and we shall wake up to the reality. But are we prepared for it?

We have to give up our pursuit of sensory objects if we seek lasting peace and joy. Material wealth brings along with it not only joy but grief as well. Accumulation of riches and multiplication of wants only lead to alternation between joy and grief. Attachment is the root of both joy and grief; detachment is the saviour.

Baba says, "Through the process of 'giving up', great things can be achieved. Cultivate detachment, and the Lord will attach Himself to you."

41

The Sage's Mouse

"When you achieve high qualifications, it promotes ego, but not humility and respect towards parents and elders."

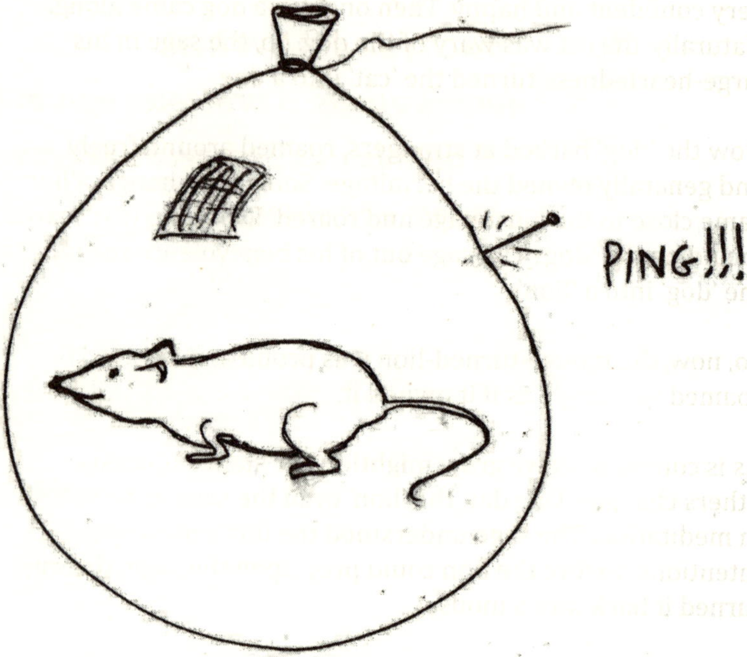
PING!!!

There once was a sage who had a pet mouse. It used to play around while the sage did his daily routine of prayers, meditation, etc. The sage was very fond of the mouse and would feed it with grains, etc.

One day the sage noticed that the mouse was scared of the cat that would sometimes be found lurking around the premises. With the strength of his mystical prowess, the sage turned the mouse into a cat. Days, passed and the 'cat' was very confident and happy. Then one day a dog came along. Naturally, the cat was wary of the dog. So, the sage in his large-heartedness turned the 'cat' into a dog.

Now the 'dog' barked at strangers, roamed around freely and generally owned the hermitage. Some days hence, a lion came close to the hermitage and roared. Everyone was scared including the 'dog'. The sage out of his benevolence turned the 'dog' into a 'lion'.

So, now, the mouse-turned-lion was proud and strong. He roamed the jungle as if it owned it.

As is common, as we grow mightier, our stance towards others changes. One day, the 'lion' eyed the sage as he sat in meditation. The sage understood the lion's mala fide intentions. Before the lion could prey upon the sage, the sage turned it back into a mouse!

The story could give you reason to smile, but if you think beyond, it has a deep meaning. Who is the mouse? It is the ego. If it becomes larger and larger; if it is fed to such an extent that it becomes too big for its own boots, it gets out of hand. It then starts questioning its own roots. If the inner voice (the sage in this case), that is the conscience, does not give it a dressing down, it can be the cause for a person's downfall.

When the human ego gets inflated, it is akin to a fully blown balloon. All you need to do is deflate it with a sharp pin! PING!!!

Do a self-check regularly. For doing a self-check, it is a good idea to look at the watch. When we look at the watch, we should reflect on the five letters of the word, WATCH and understand the life lessons it gives us:

'W' warns you to — Watch your Words

'A' advises you to — Watch your Actions

'T' tells you to — Watch your Thoughts

'C' cautions you to — Watch your Character

'H' heeds you to — Watch your Heart

So, next time and every time, when you look at your watch, do pause and think about the lesson that the watch is imparting!

42

The Best Gift

"Your parents work very hard to feed you, educate you and bring you up in life. They struggle to keep you in good mood and give you good food, good clothing and good education. If you do not respect such parents, how do you expect to be respected by society? You must bring joy to your parents through your behaviour."

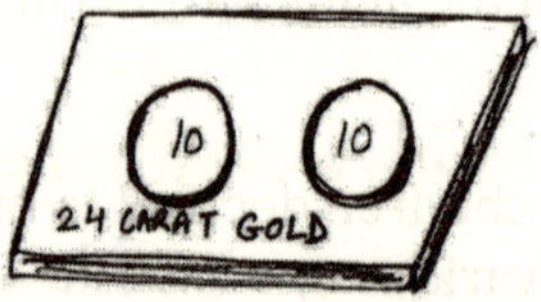
10
10
24 CARAT GOLD

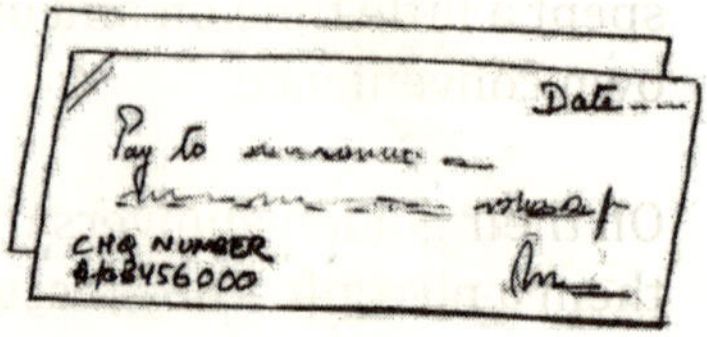
Date
Pay to
CHQ NUMBER

A couple had grown old. They were failing health. As usually happens in old age, both had health issues, some serious, others trivial. They still had their share of arguments but they were both dependent on each other's presence. With God's grace, they were well off. They were not dependent on their three sons and a daughter.

Each of the four children were busy in their own lives and spent a little time on and off with the aging parents at their own convenience.

On their golden anniversary, the children decided to give them a nice gift. They discussed various options but were not able to come to a consensus. So, eventually, each decided to go his own way.

The eldest son gave them a gold coin each. He said that they could buy anything they wanted in exchange for the coins that were worth a good sum. The second son transferred a tidy sum of money into the bank accounts of the mother and the father. He felt mighty pleased with his gesture.

The third son gave them an offer for a holiday anywhere in the world, saying that he would be happy to foot the bill of the holiday, whatever it may be.

The daughter was not so well off. All she could afford was a simple cotton shirt for the mother and a *kurta* for her father. So, she gave them just that. The cotton shirt and *kurta* were worn and washed umpteen times. The daughter visited the parents every other day. She called them up and spoke to them if she could not visit. She gave them the gift of her time!

A year or so later, the mother died and the father died soon after. The gold coins lay in the safe as they were. The money too lay unspent, in the savings bank accounts and, of course the, holiday never happened because they were never well enough to do it.

Simple and inexpensive gifts are perhaps the best. It's not the value of the gift that matters. It's the thought behind it that is of value.

When children are small, the parents are young. That is the time the parents want to build their careers by working long hours. If they are affluently placed, they want to enjoy life, go places, party, travel, socialise, etc. But this is also the time when babies need their parents. The way a mother can bring up a child, a nanny cannot. Sacrifices made by parents at this stage surely bear fruit. Our parents' generation made so many sacrifices for us. I wonder why parenting seems to be going out of fashion. I guess there is no harm in having maids or servants or other help too, for but my sincere advice to all young parents is — do find time for your children ...

Conversely, if you have aged parents, do make it a point to pay-rent to them. Pay them the RENT of Respect, Empathy, Niceness and Time!!!

Having received so much from them, including the biggest gift, which is the gift of life, is it too much that we give something to them?

All said and done, the best gifts you can give to your aged parents are your time and some gratitude. Conversely, the best gift young parents can give to their babies is their time and lots of love.

Life is all about give and take! You give some; you get some.

43

King for 5 Years

"Goodness in this world and Godliness for the life after death — equal attention needs to be given to both. One must be vigilant while taking a step, whichever foot it may be. Both are essential for a happy journey through life."

There was a precedent in a small province that the king was elected for a period of five years. Thereafter, he was sent to the jungle. Once the five years were over, he had to fend for himself. He could take nothing along. No money, food, shelter, clothing, servants not even family. It was a strange custom, but it had been prevalent since long.

The former king in the jungle would eventually be consumed by the hunger of wild animals or the harshness of the elements.

One particular king, when he was coronated to the throne, thought about what would happen to him five years hence. In the years while he was in power, he got the neighbouring jungle cleared of carnivorous animals. He got a comfortable guest house built there. He got sufficient clothing and bedding placed for a long time to come. A well was dug for drinking water. Some fruit trees, edible greens and legumes were planted around the vicinity. When his term as king was over, he happily went to the retreat he had prepared for himself and lived there comfortably and spent his time in prayer and meditation.

The story has a powerful message. While we are young and able, we should make arrangements for our old age. Plan your finances such that you have enough to support you, when you can no longer earn. It is unwise to 'Eat, drink and be merry, for tomorrow you might die!'

Here is another perspective, a millionaire pays income-tax with tears in his eyes; a headmaster joyfully gives up the furniture and laboratory appliances of his school when he is transferred to some other place or retires from service. Why? Because the headmaster knows that he is only the caretaker, not the owner. He is not attached to these articles; he knows that they belong to the government. So, too, feel that your family, house, property, car, etc. are all the Lord's property and that you are only the trustee, be ready to give them up without a murmur at a moment's notice.

On a spiritual plane too, our sacred scriptures contain the drugs to cure attachment and endow you with the strength of detachment.

Sacrifice *(Tyaga)* does not mean that you should not value things, or that you should not care for them. We just need to constantly remember that they are transient, that the joy they give is trivial and temporary. We need to understand their real worth and not over-estimate them. We need to stay unattached from them, at the same time, accumulate good *karma* so that our after-life is taken care of.

Perhaps we can think of the five years of the king as the last five years of our life. We should leave attachments and spend time in doing good deeds, helping others and praying, etc. But how does one know when it is that the last five years commence?

There is no way to know. So, the only way is to do good *karma* and walk the right path each day of our lives. Who knows when our call may come?

It would do good to remember that the merits of the good deeds we do in this world shall be available to us in the next!

44

EQUIPOISE

"Pain and pleasure, sorrow and happiness follow one another. One should treat them with equanimity." — BABA

-ve

+ve

A rich man was heading a business that was quite turbulent in the present day. As in all business, there were good times and bad times. So, presently, the business was not good. But the man maintained his equanimity and poise in all circumstances.

One of his employees, his personal secretary was an emotional man who got disturbed easily. He was under a lot of stress due to the ups and downs happening everyday. One day he asked his Boss, "Sir, how come you are able to maintain your calm? Yesterday our biggest client withdrew the business. Payments are pending from so many clients but you remain unperturbed. How is it possible to remain unaffected? Is it that you don't get disturbed at all or do you hide your emotions and maintain a perfect plastic face in public?"

The man said, "I am able to do so because I study palmistry too. Perhaps you don't know. Here show me your hand. Let's see what life has in store for you."

So, the secretary extended his palm for the boss to 'read' He said, 'Oh my God! You are going to die in five days. Your life is almost over! Oh! That's very sad! Is there anything else you want to ask me?" The secretary was stupefied, stunned and totally dumb-struck. What was there to ask now? He quickly excused himself and went home.

He told the news to his wife. He quickly wrote out a Will. He lay down in bed saying that he was feeling unwell. As the days passed, he became more unwell and quiet. He lay down in the bed and kept his eyes closed most of the time.

As day five was drawing to an end, his wife and daughter started crying. He started breathing heavily. He too had tears in his eyes.

Just then the doorbell rang. The boss came in. He said, "How are you?" The man said feebly, "Preparing to go Sir."

The boss smiled, "In these five days, have you had any anxiety or thought about any of the problems of the business? Have you committed any sin or fraud?"

"How could I, Sir? I have spent these five days in prayer. I have been preparing for my last journey. Death has been on my mind every moment."

The boss said, "That is the state of mind I maintain, my friend. That is why I keep my equanimity; my equipoise. Death is certain, we all know it. But we keep postponing the thought from our minds. As for you, you have many more years to live. Get up! There is nothing wrong with you!"

The man sat up with a start! He said, "But you said I am going to die."

"That my friend was the only way to answer your question. Now get up and get going!"

"But you said you knew, because you knew about Palmistry!"

"Just gimmicks, my friend! The only thing I know about palms is that we should fold them in prayer every morning and evening!"

Gone was the illness! The man was fit as a fiddle!

They say the greatest wonder is that everyday death strikes, yet man lives as though he is immortal.

Living in the awareness that the 'call' from the Lord may come anytime makes us abstain from doing wrong. If we live in the awareness that the Lord is watching us and listening to us, we can never go wrong!

45

Donation

"Your mind can build a silent refuge or tie you up into complex knots. It binds; it loosens bonds. You can sail safe on the sea of worldly life (samsaar), if you have no leaks in the boat; but through the leaks of lust, anger, greed, delusion, pride and envy (kamakrodha, lobha, moha, mada and matsarya), the waters of the worldly life will enter the boat and it will sink, drowning you beyond redemption. Stop all the leaks!"

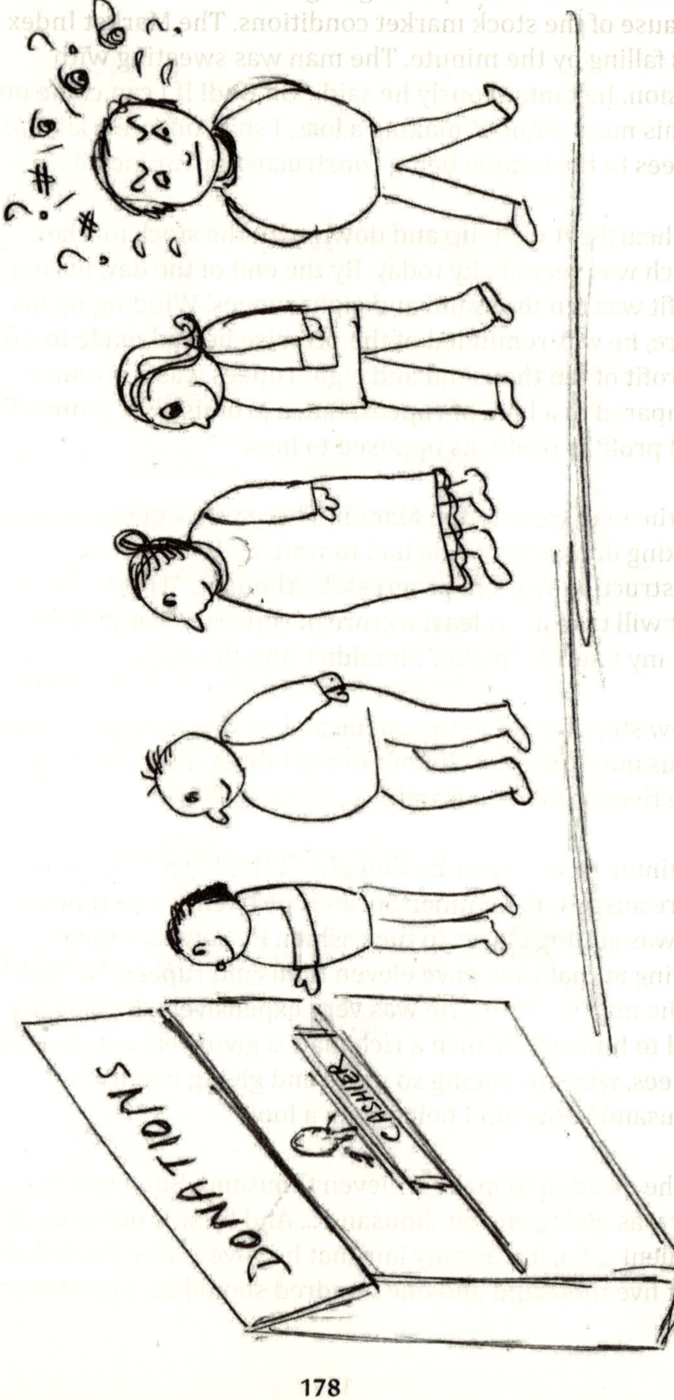
DONATIONS
CASHIER

A stock broker was expecting huge losses in his business, because of the stock market conditions. The Market Index was falling by the minute. The man was sweating with tension. Instantaneously he said, "Oh God! If I can come out of this mess without making a loss, I shall donate a lakh of rupees to the temple being constructed in our locality."

His heartbeat went up and down with the stock market, which was very shaky today. By the end of the day, his net profit was ten thousand and eight rupees. Winding up his office, he was reminded of the promise he had made to God. A profit of ten thousand and eight rupees was a pittance compared to a lakh of rupees. But, a promise is a promise. And profit is profit, as opposed to loss.

So, the man went to the Mandir. There was a queue of people, making donations, so he had to wait. As he watched the construction work in progress, he thought, "This is a project that will take up at least a crore of rupees. What difference will my one lakh make? Shouldn't fifty thousand be enough?"

A few steps ahead in the queue and he thought, "Actually, fifty thousand rupees is a lot of money. I think it should be fine to give twenty-five thousand."

A minute or two later he thought, "I think twenty-one is a more auspicious number. So, let it be twenty-one thousand." He was getting closer to the cashier. He saw that the man paying at that time gave eleven thousand rupees. He looked at the man's clothes. He was very expensively dressed. He said to himself, "If such a rich man is giving eleven thousand rupees, why am I being so naïve and giving twenty-one thousand? Why am I being such a fool?"

So, he decided to make it eleven thousand. But, even that rich guy was giving eleven thousand ... And he was not even as affluent ... So, it was only fair that he gave lesser. He decided that five thousand and one hundred should be a good amount to give. He was almost there now. There was just one person ahead of him.

As he drew out the currency notes from his wallet, he saw his boss there. He was holding a receipt for two thousand one hundred. Oh! The boss is giving just two thousand one hundred! Why should I fritter away my hard-earned money? I think I should also give two thousand one hundred. And, it's not like I didn't work hard to save my situation in the volatility of the stock market situation. Come to think of it, wouldn't it be enough to donate ten percent of the profit I earned? In that case a, thousand rupees is all that is due. But, actually, a thousand is not really an auspicious number. Should I make it eleven hundred? A thousand? Eleven hundred?"

By then, he stood facing the cashier. "Yes sir! How much would you like to donate?" The man was so confused by now that he said, "Excuse me, I will just be back. I need to go to the washroom urgently."

He moved out of the queue. He thought, "What is the point of giving a thousand rupees? Who would even notice it? It would be a drop in the ocean. Actually, if I have to give something, it should be lakh only. But I can't afford it today. So, it is better I do it another time." So, the man left without shelling out a *paisa*.

If you feel like doing a good deed, or like donating something or helping somebody, just do it right away. Who knows when you would change your mind? And then it would be an opportunity lost.

46

Just Pour It Into The River

"The body is like a water bubble. The mind is like a mad monkey. If you follow this mad monkey, you will get into trouble. In the same manner, if you believe in the body, you do not know when this body, which is like a water bubble, will burst."

A man was having a stress-filled day. In modern times, this is quite a common place. Everyone has stress related to work, family, finances, relationships, etc. Perhaps we expect too much from those around us as well as from ourselves. Perhaps we set our targets too high and they, in turn, give us stress. Perhaps we are trying to achieve too much, in too little time. I wonder what we are trying to prove to ourselves or to the world! Perhaps we need to slow down ...

So, this man went to a wise elder to ask for help. The wise man heard his woes and said, "My friend, your problem is simple. Here, take this spoonful of salt. Mix it in a glass of water and drink it." The man did as directed. The salt water was terribly unpalatable, but somehow he drank it all up. The wise man asked, "How did that taste?" "Horrible!" he said.

The wise man gave him another spoon of salt and told him to mix it in a glass of water and drink it. The man was flabbergasted. He began to sip the salt water. If possible, it tasted even worse than the earlier one. Half way through he threw up. He said, "I can't, I can't drink more. Please do not play jokes with me. I came to seek help from you. Why are you doing this to me?" The wise man said, "Alright, take the rest of the salt water and pour it into the river yonder. Then mix it and fill up a glass from there and bring it."

The man did as he was told. "Now, drink it," said the wise man. The man drank it easily. "How did it taste?" "Very cool and refreshing," he replied. "Do you understand what to do now?"

The man shook his head, "No," he said. The wise man explained, "All the problems that you have recounted to me are of the present. Their nature is temporary. They affect you so much because your vision is centred only on them. Look at the larger picture. Think of these problems as a small speck in the happenings of the day in the master plan of the universe. Look around and count your blessings. If you see your problems in perspective against the larger plan of the Lord, you shall realise that the problems are but dust particles that shall soon drift away."

Similarly, once a king, his minister and servant going in a boat. The servant panicked at the sight of water all round; in fact, his panic tantrums were about to upset the boat itself. So, the minister caught hold of him, dunked him into the water, dipped him a number of times and then when he cried, "The boat, the boat!" he was hoisted back. Once in the boat, he knew he was safe from the stormy waters.

Do not panic unnecessarily and create mountains out of molehills. Problems will come and go, what matters is how you deal with them. What matters is whether you can maintain your equanimity in all circumstances.

We need to learn to be serene and calm in stress and storm. The mind is a wanderer. Wandering from wish to wish, flitting from one desire to another is its nature. It causes loss and grief, elation and depression. Its effects are both positive and negative. The mind will gather experiences and store them in the memory forever. It does not know the art of giving up! As a consequence, grief, anxiety and misery continue simmering in it. It is worthwhile to know the characteristics of our mind and the ways to master it, for we shall ultimately benefit from the exercise!

47

Food For God

"Poornamadah Poornamidam
Poornaath Poomamudachyathe
Poornasya Poornamaadaaya
Poornameva Vasishyathe.

Means—
The perfect whole is the basis. All that is here is the perfect whole. The whole emanates from the whole. When the whole is separated from the whole, the perfect wholeness remains perfect as wholeness."

Every Sunday, we as a family sit in our Mandir at home and sing *Bhajans* and read a few pages from any scriptural text. These days we are reading from the Bhagwad Puran.

I placed the bowl of fruit to be offered to the Lord on the shelf of the Mandir. My niece who was visiting asked me, "Does He really eat it?" I nodded in affirmation. "If He really eats it, then how come the quantity is not reduced? I smiled and said, "We shall talk after we finish our Mandir session." All through, the Bhajan and the reading of the Bhagwad Puran, my mind was nagged by the question posed by my young niece. I prayed to the Lord to throw some light on the issue. Not that I doubted if He partook of the offering. Of that I was convinced. But, how should I satisfy her? How could I explain it to her?"

After Sanjay finished reading the Bhagwad, he said, "Can any of you retell the story that we just read?" Before our children could so much as open their mouths to offer, our overenthusiastic little niece said excitedly, "Rishi Gautam had gone for a bath and Indra disguised himself as Gautam and came to meet Ahilya. She thought it was her husband. And, later, when she came to know that she had been tricked, she cursed Indra."

So spontaneous and clear-headed was her simple narrative that she bowled all of us over. And like a spark, the Lord gave me the answer.

Later, I sat with her and asked, "You narrated the story of Ahilya very well. From where did you learn it?" She looked at me incredulously and said, "Sanjay uncle, read it out from the Bhagwad Puran. Were you not listening attentively?" I smiled and said, "So you got it from there ... Hmm." She nodded vigorously. "But, the Bhagwad Puran is still lying there. If you took away so much learning from it, how is it still there in its original form?" She looked thoughtful.

"In the same way, when we offer food to the Lord. He partakes of it. We offer it in its gross form, but He partakes of it in its subtle form. He partakes of the feeling and devotion with which it is offered. So, the physical quantity remains to be the same. Love and devotion, learning and emotion cannot be seen, but they are for real!"

Really speaking, do you think God needs anything at all? Even offering food to Him is more for us; it is a way to give form and shape to our emotion of devotion. If we do it with love, we feel blessed. If we do it just as a ritual and there is no feeling involved, there is no feeling of bliss. So, eventually, we are the ones who stand to benefit by experiencing bliss!

Reflect on this — Everyday, the whole world takes light and warmth from the Sun; has it diminished in size? For aeons, the Earth has produced trees, plants, fruits, vegetables ... has the size of the Earth reduced? God never reduces or increases in size. God is. Period!

Dear Reader, we feel blessed that we are a family that prays together. Every Sunday, we collectively spend about an hour in our Mandir, reading and singing the glory of the Lord.

Baba tells us that a home must be filled with love. Any brick and mortar structure where parents and children spend their lives cannot be a home if children do not yearn for it, and if parents do not find peace therein. The home is the temple where each member is nurtured and nourished. Humility is the incense with which the house is filled. Reverence is the lamp that is lit with love as the oil and faith as the wick.

48

Lassi

"Human beings alone have the quality of empathy; they alone can be happy when others are happy, and miserable when others are miserable. That is why, human beings are the paragon of all creation."

It was a hot summer day and the Sun was shining bright. Stopping at a way side *Dhaba* (eatery) while travelling from Chandigarh to Amritsar, a man was enjoying a tall glass of *Lassi* which is a speciality of the state of Punjab. It is made by churning curd made of full-cream milk with loads of sugar and ice. It is served topped with *malai* (cream of milk).

An old woman was begging at the *Dhaba* which was as per tradition an open air eatery. The man dug into his pocket to fish out a coin or two. All of a sudden he said, "Amma, will you have *Lassi*?" His family looked at him incredulously. The old woman looked dumb-struck. The man repeated, "Amma, would you like to have *Lassi*?" The *Lassi* would cost no less than fifty bucks. The old woman opened her fist to reveal some seven-eight rupees and said, "This is all I have collected today. If you will pay the rest, I will have the *Lassi*."

The man patted her rough and wrinkled hand as if to tell her to keep her bounty. He ordered a *Lassi* for her. When it came, he realised that he could not ask her to sit and drink on the same table, for it may be inappropriate. So, he asked her to sit on the floor alongside and proceeded to sit cross-legged beside her on the floor.

The owner of the restaurant was watching the scene. He came and said, "Sir, please be seated on the chair. Ammaji, you also sit on the chair. Here, let me help you." So saying, the owner held the glass of *Lassi*, while the old woman slowly got up; straightened her back and carefully stepped towards the chair."

The look on the face of the old woman wouldn't be difficult to imagine ... Needless to say, the old woman drank the *lassi* as if it was nectar. She showered blessings from her heart on the man. What effect do you think this had on the owner of the *Dhaba?* Since then, he vowed to give at least two glasses of *Lassi* every day to a beggar that passed that way.

Think about this — The *Dhaba* owner had the means to do charity since long. There would have been many beggars around too. But, why did he start doing this good deed now? Because he got inspired seeing another do it! Sometimes we need a wake-up call. Sometimes someone needs to shake us to wake us. There is no paucity of goodness in this world. But selfishness and self-centredness has just become a way of life. Seldom do we try to feel the hunger pangs of a fellow human being. Helping others is not just for their sake, but it is also a course in self-evolution.

There are so many people who are affluent and capable of sharing. But, they don't think of it because they are too busy doing their own thing.

Let me share here for the sole purpose of inspiring others ... our father Sh. Balramji Dass Tandon is presently the Governor of Chhattisgarh state. He draws a salary of `1.1 lakhs. In the month of June 2018, it was announced that the salary has been increased from `1.1 to `3.5 lakhs per month with retrospective effect from 1.1.2016. He refused to take the arrears as well as the hiked emolument for the coming period. Why? Who says 'No' to such a declaration of payment of wages? He is of the view that in the twilight years of his life, his needs are limited. Whatever he has is sufficient to meet his needs and he is content with what he has!

I hope that this spirit of contentment and absence of greed continue to inspire the present and future generations of our family and is an inspiration for others too.

49

The Oil in the Lamp

"Remember, Seva (service) is more fruitful than japa, dhyana, yajna and yaga (recitations, meditation, sacrifices and rituals) usually recommended for spiritual aspirants. For, it serves two purposes: the extinction of the ego, and the attainment of ananda (bliss)."

A lamp was burning to dispel the darkness. It contained a layer of oil floating over water. The water filled a large portion of the lamp. There was a conversation between the oil and the water. Do tune in –

Water : I am purer than you. Why is it that you get to float over me always? I am superior to you in every way.

Oil : I have been through many hardships to reach where I am today. Do you know that I was born in a field? I grew as a seed on a plant that endured the vagaries of the seasons, standing in the field. When all the seeds on my mother plant were ripe, the plant was uprooted and beaten and thrashed to dislodge all the seeds. Oh! How painful it was! Later, all the seeds were collected and pressed in a machine so that the oil came out. I have been through a rigorous process of pain to become what I am.

Water : Wow! I never thought of that.

Oil : And look at me now. I am burning myself to give light. I am being consumed to light up this room. Soon I shall be no more. For all that, do you still grudge my position to be laid above you?

Water : No, my friend. I realise your pain and value your spirit of self-sacrifice. Let me have the honour of holding you high on my shoulders till your last drop!!!

Everything happens for a reason, even if it is a thing as simple as why oil floats over water, if only we care to gaze yonder and try to understand. The scientist would tell it in a different way, saying that the density of oil is lesser than that of water, hence, it floats over water, but sometimes the spiritual significance holds a lesson or two!

Thinking at a tangent, human life is the most coveted of all living beings. Humans are the highest form of God's creation.

So, should we too not let ourselves be consumed in the service of others?

Baba says that we should make everyday a continuous offering of love, like an oil lamp that exhausts itself in illumining its surroundings. We should wear the invisible badge of a volunteer of God at all hours and in all places. Bend the body, mend the senses, and end the mind — that is the process of attaining the status of 'the children of immortality', which the Upanishads talk about.

50

Yummy Golgappas

"Divine Life is based on the quality of calm serenity (satwaguna), which must be cultivated. This quality can be built only upon satwic food — food that promotes health, strength, lightness of spirit, and earnestness of endeavour."

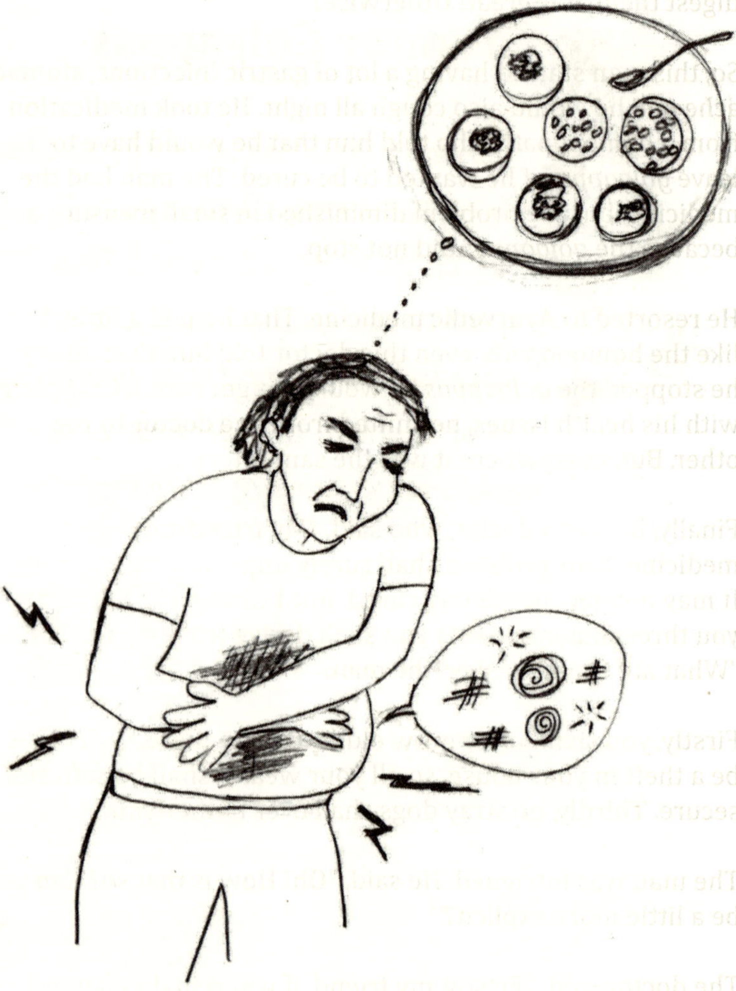

A man was very fond of eating *golgappas/pani-puri*. Such was his addiction for them that every evening on his way home from work, he would stop by the *golgappa* shop and have at least ten of them.

Well, a lot of people have *golgappas,* but, if one is able to digest them, it is great! Otherwise?

So, this man started having a lot of gastric infections, stomach ache and he would also cough all night. He took medication from a homoeopath who told him that he would have to leave *golgappas* if he wanted to be cured. The man had the medicine, but the problem diminished in small measure only because the *golgappas* did not stop.

He resorted to Ayurvedic medicine. That helped a little, but like the homoeopath, even this doctor told him that unless he stopped the *golgappas* he would not get cured. Grappling with his health issues, he shifted from one doctor to the other. But, everywhere it was the same story.

Finally, he met a doctor, who said, "My friend, take this medicine. Your problem shall surely improve considerably. It may not get completely cured. But I can surely guarantee you three major benefits you shall derive from my medicine." "What are those?" asked the man.

Firstly, you shall never grow old. Secondly, there shall never be a theft in your house, so all your wealth shall be safe and secure. Thirdly, no stray dogs shall ever bother you."

The man was intrigued. He said, "Oh! How is that so? Can you be a little more explicit?"

The doctor said, "Firstly, my friend, if you remain plagued continually by gastric infections, etc., you shall surely die young; so you shall never ever grow old!

Secondly, your horse-like cough shall keep not only you awake at night, It shall also caution all potential burglars that you are awake. So, no thief shall ever venture into your house at night.

Thirdly, my friend, you shall soon need a stick to walk with, for your body shall become weak with constant coughing. So, when you have a stick in hand, why would a stray dog come near you?"

Phew! Surely, he said it all. Do you know who lost a regular customer from the very next day? Yes!

Baba tells us that if you persist in giving yourself simple food that is not savoury or hot, but amply sustaining, the tongue may squirm for a few days, but it will soon welcome it. That is the way to subdue it and overcome the evil consequences of it being your master.

51

The Debt of Haridas

"Scriptures declare: Revere the mother and father as God. Mother's womb is the birthplace of one and all, be it a commoner or the Avatar Himself. Therefore, adore the mother as God. There is nothing greater than mother's love."

There was a poor village boy whose mother was a widow and did menial chores in the houses of rich landlords. A monk came to their village along with his many disciples. Since he was to stay for a few months, the villagers amongst other arrangements deputed this boy of 10 years to help out with the Guru's errands and chores.

The boy dutifully rose at dawn before the Guru and cleaned and swept the place. He brought flowers and *Tulsi* leaves for the morning prayers. The Guru would do *Pravachan* in the morning and *Bhajan-Keertanam* and *Naam-Smaranam* in the evening. The villagers attended his sessions very keenly and all of them enjoyed the bliss. The boy, by his devout attention to the needs of the Guru, pleased the ascetic. He named the boy 'Haridas'.

Haridas one day was cleaning the place when the Guru asked him if he had eaten yet. The boy replied that he had not. The Guru gave him *prasadam* from his own plate. The boy became totally immersed in the bliss of *Nama Samarana*. He spent his day in doing *seva* to the Guru and chanting the name of Krishna.

After a few months, the Guru decided to move on. The boy was by now very attached to the Guru and could not bear the thought of being left behind. So, he begged the Guru to take him along. The Guru said, "If I take you with me, who will look after your mother? You have a debt to pay to the mother who gave birth to you. You have to do your duty towards her. Stay here and continue your *Nama-Smarana*. Any worldly mother would want her son to get married and have children, and so will your mother. She will not be happy by your becoming so attached to God.

But, you do not have to give up the path of *Bhakti*. But, never insult your mother. Always be respectful to her. Who knows, God may find a way out for you. She may even become a *Bhakta* herself."

The boy was not willing to be left behind. He said, "Guruji, in your discourse, you said that if anyone comes between you and God, you should shun him. In my case, my mother is hampering my relationship with my Krishna. So, why should I not leave her? Take me with you please."

The Guru said, "My child, if you desert your mother, and come with us, her cries and longing for you shall disturb our penance. You must discharge your duty first. Only then can you be free of any ties. If you don't, you will have to be born again to discharge your obligation towards your mother."

So, the Guru went away and the boy cried bitterly. But, he did not give up the discipline of Nama-Smarana. For twelve years, he meditated and sung the glory of Krishna. He performed all his worldly duties towards his mother.

One day while she was cleaning the cowshed, a snake bit her and she died. Haridas performed her last rites and was at peace that he had completed his worldly duty towards the mother of his physical body. Without taking anything from her belongings in the house, he left home and visited many holy places and sung the glory of the Lord.

After another twelve years of living in complete discipline, while meditating at the shore of the Ganges, he shed his mortal coil.

The story says that due to the merits of his *seva* and *Nama smarana,* he was reborn as the son of Brahma and is known to us as Narada.

The point that really caught my attention while reading this little story in the Bhagwad Puran is the emphasis laid by the Guru on duty. Think a while on this... and reflect on its profundity!

52

Sab Mein Ram

"The divinity within is covered by ego and anger. Therefore, it is said, real knowledge dawns only when attachment is destroyed."

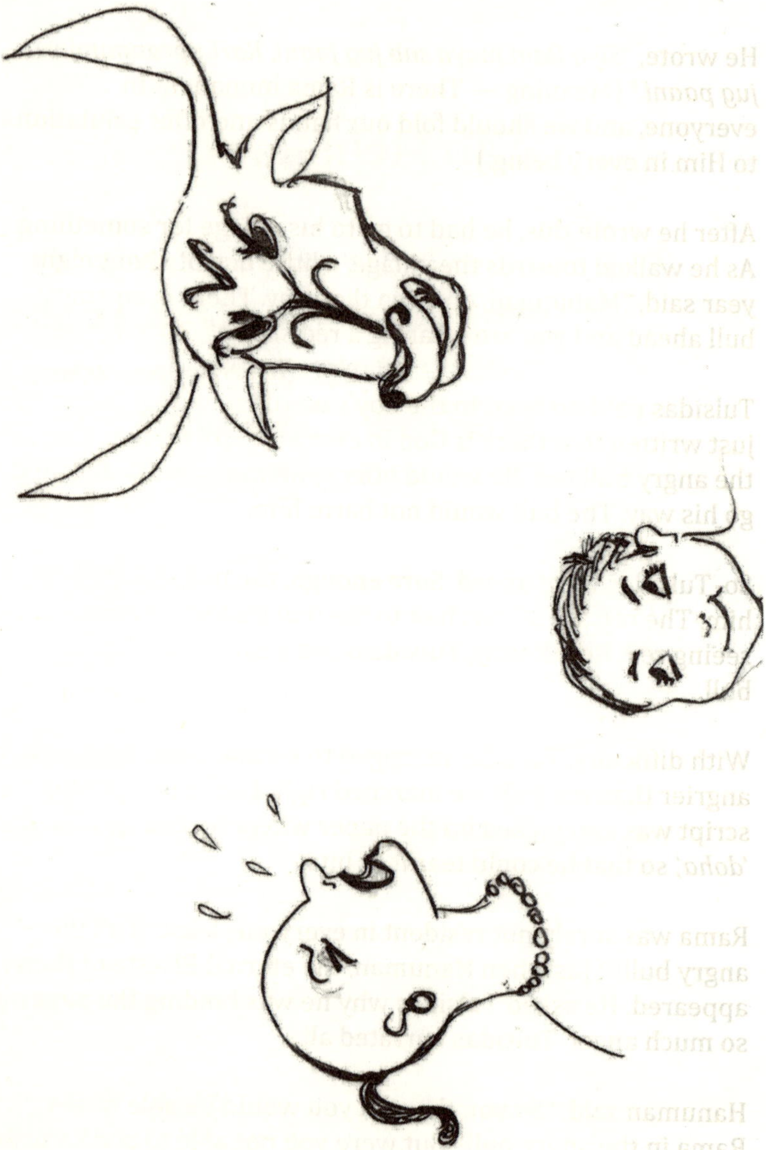

Tulsidas, the great Saint who wrote the Ramayana, wrote it as if he could hear the Lord dictate it to him. He wrote it in flow, like the verses of a poem. He did not have to think and write; he just wrote and wrote...

He wrote, *"Siya Ram maya sab jag Jaani, Karhupranaamjori jug paani."* (Meaning — There is Rama immanent in everyone, and we should fold our hands and offer salutations to Him in every being.)

After he wrote this, he had to go to his village for something. As he walked towards the village, a little boy of about eight year said, "Mahatmaji, don't go that way. There is an angry bull ahead and you are wearing a red shawl."

Tulsidas paid no heed to the boy's words thinking that he had just written that there is God in everyone. So, there is God in the angry bull too. He would offer salutations to the bull and go his way. The bull would not harm him.

So, Tulsidas went ahead. Sure enough, the bull charged at him. The red shawl was bait to the bull that was already seeing red. Resultantly, Tulsidass got a battering from the bull.

With difficulty, Tulsidas managed to escape alive. Now he was angrier than the bull. He marched right back to where his script was and picked up the paper where he had written the *'doha',* so that he could tear it to bits.

Rama was surely not resident in everyone, least of all the angry bull!!! Just then Hanuman, the eternal Bhakta of Rama appeared. He asked Tulsidas why he was holding the paper in so much anger. Tulsidas narrated all.

Hanuman said, "So you thought you would be able to see Rama in the angry bull? But were you not able to see Rama in the little boy that warned you to not go that way?"

No one is too small to be overlooked as inconsequential. God is surely resident in all.

In this world, every being is an embodiment of Divinity. Whomsoever you salute, it reaches God! Likewise, whomsoever you criticise, the criticism too reaches God. At the same time, man alone has been given the power of discrimination and discernment. Usage of the intellect is wholly and solely restricted to humans, which are the paragon of God's creation.

Bhagwan Baba tells us that God is present in all, but each creature acts and does according to its innate nature. Don't discard your ability to think and discriminate. If you let yourself into a lion's cage or into the hole of a snake, what do you expect?

GRATITUDE OH LORD!

Thank you Lord for letting us feel,
The love and the grace that flows for free!

The tear in the eye,
The cloud in the sky...

The warmth in the gaze,
The sadness in the haze...

The beauty in belief,
The surrender in relief...

The blush on the rose,
The poetry in the prose...

The passion in compassion,
The grace in adulation...

The beat of the heart,
The creation of an art...

Thank you Lord! For letting us feel,
The love and the grace that flows through Thee!

AFTER WORD

This book is literally a download of the thoughts resonating and floating in the Cosmos. We have been the blessed ones who were able to tune in and be the medium through which the 'download' happened.

Despite utmost care having been given to not hurt the sentiment of any person or people, in case any such material has crept in, that has caused hurt to anyone, we offer our apologies for the same. This book is made to just give love, share love and spread love.

The more you share, the more there is to share!

Keep smiling. It's the best thing you can do for yourself and for others. It makes people wonder what you have within and is the best way of accepting your lot with love and humility. Don't ever forget that God loves you, no matter what...

— Priya and Sanjay Tandon

EXCERPTS FROM SOME LETTERS RECEIVED BY US

"The Sunrays series of books to me are a harbinger of positivity and good thoughts. I think such books are tremendously necessary in today's world where finding a positive piece of text is a luxury. These books infuse a little glimmer of hope in your day by their short, crisp and value oriented stories. I would like to give my blessings and good wishes to Priya and Sanjay who continue to bring positivity to our life and inspire us every single day. May the flow of goodness continue!"

— Dr. Ashok Khanna

Chairman: Khanna Watches Ltd. & Khanna Infrastructures
Past President: PHD Chamber
Former Managing Committee Member: ASSOCHAM, CII & FICCI
Founder Chairman, Art of Living, Apex Body
(Chandigarh, Haryana, Himachal Pradesh & Punjab)

"Sunrays series of books by Priya and Sanjay Tandon indeed is a unique idea. Initially, it started with bringing together stories we heard from our grandparents to inculcate moral and social values in us. It was indeed a great effort to apprise the current generation about moral and social values through these age-old, tried and tested fables. Stories that had been forgotten got revived and the book became popular among both elderly and youngsters, alike. The subsequent volumes added on to the effort with the authors penning down own stories based on their life experiences and helped spread the good word further."

— Desh Deepak Khanna

Editor & Publisher, Exam Resource Online

"Over the last couple of years, one has been enriched by the daily thoughts, story of the week and the series of Sunrays books which you have so graciously sent to me. I must confess that this association has made a real impact on me both personally and professionally. Some of the basics like being truthful, caring, respect and kindness for weak and elders come to your readers through constant reinforcements. Please continue to be a part of my life."

— Sandeep Bakshi
COO, ICICI Bank Ltd.

When I received the first copy of the book 'Sunrays', authored by Sanjay and Priya, I was on the way to Shimla. As the car drove up the hills, I held the book in my hand, an old habit to become one with the book. There was fog all around as I gingerly opened the book. The first write-up, part anecdotal, part didactic and immensely inspirational lifted my spirits. The fog gave way to bright sunshine. Since then, I have read the 'Sunrays' series, sometimes a page at a time and sometimes at a stretch. These books are natural outpourings of two evolved souls who with their writings spread happiness, love and joy. May they keep writing and sharing.

— Sheel Vardhan Singh, IPS

The 'Sunrays' series are presented by the authors as inspirational stories. A few lines of distilled wisdom precede each story that fires up the readers' mind, while accompanying minimalist sketches create the right mental context for delving into the story. Every story ends by reinforcing the underlying idea. The format is ideal for making the readers reflect and retain what they read. Given the need to inculcate ethical and prudent conduct in a fast atomising society, the likes of IIMs or ISBs could do well to position these stories as timeless management principles that impart an edge in life and business.

— Anil Kishora
DMD, State Bank of India

"The stories read by me and my family has helped us in changing our attitude, habits, thinking positively and the real purpose of our life. It transforms the paradigm of an average individual and can make his life count. I am a big believer of God and this book has strengthened my belief that God really bleses and loves us."

— Parveen Gandhi
Managing Director, Indo-Sing Business Advisory Pvt. Ltd.

"I have been privileged to read Sunrays for Saturday right from the first edition and it's been truly inspiring. I use the book to read pages whenever I have spiritual gathering at my place. I am grateful to Sanjay and Priya for putting in ardent efforts in compiling the book. My best wishes and love as always."

— Raj Bhatt

Chairman & CEO, Elara Capital Advisors Ltd.

"When I first put my hands on Sunrays for Sunday, I read it through till the end. It was unputdownable. So are all the other books in the series. Each time I get the new one, I have to read it at one go. The stories are so familiar, yet so enthralling. I am transported back to the days when mum and dad related them as our daily dose of learning and love from the parents. I remember the happy expressions on the faces of my children when little, as I related some of these stories to them. And yet there are so many new ones in the books which I enjoy reading from time to time.

I am so proud of you for penning them down for the world and future generations to benefit. I have also endeavoured to gift at least one book to friends and relatives who I visit. I must have distributed hundreds. It's a perfect and well-appreciated gift for any age.

Each recipient has beautiful things to say which makes me even more proud of you. Keep the pen going and let the world benefit."

— Madhu Mutneja

"The life of a professional cricketer involves many ups and downs. There is a lot of pressure and we're expected to succeed every time we take the field. The failures test our mental toughness and self-belief, and at such times, some positivity from friends, family, movies, books, etc. goes a long way. I try to stay positive, and keep a "it's not over till I succeed" mentality.

I have known the Tandon family for many years, and whenever I have referred to the Sunrays books, I have drawn some positivity from them. I am sure the readers will feel good vibes while reading them."

— Manan Vohra

Royal Challengers Bangalore, IPL

EXCERPTS FROM THE PRESS COVERAGE ABOUT SUNRAYS FOR FRIDAY

THE TRIBUNE LIFE + STYLE PUBLICATION

"Rays of divinity...

Sanjay Tandon and his wife have culled out the best of Sri Sathya Sai Baba's teachings in their book Sunrays for Friday, the sixth in the Sunrays collection.

It all commenced with an urge to kindle the latent spark of human values in kindred spirits... my spouse and I decided to weave short stories (the Sunrise series) around Baba's teachings. The idea being to usher-in a revival of human values... to shed light on the power of the written word, and more importantly, story-telling.

The Sunrays series, are the couple's "offerings to Baba", contain 52 short stories. "I write a story's first draft. We hold discussions over each tale and modify accordingly. And then I sketch illustrations to go with the written matter," says Priya.

The couple, which puts pen to paper with the intent of illumining their readers' world with 'sunrays' full of positive thoughts, shares that "all proceeds from the sale of these books go to charity."

What's more, with their bouquet of thoughts, the duo wishes to subtly touch the lives of people not only from different walks of life, but varied age groups too, for they believe that "Right from an eight-year-old kid to an 80-year-old man, each one of us is a learner for life!"

HINDUSTAN TIMES NEWS —

The Union health minister, J.P. Nadda and Haryana Chief Minister M.L. Khattar on Saturday released the book 'Sunrays for Friday' authored by Bharatiya Janata Party (BJP) UT Chief, Sanjay Tandon and his wife, Priya Tandon at Law Bhawan in Sector-37.

The book series, a collection of short stories is sixth book by the couple. Speaking on the occasion, Nadda lauded the efforts of Competent Foundation, an NGO, run by Tandon family in organising blood camps, eye donation camps, disposal of unclaimed bodies and contributing towards other social causes. Khattar shared about his bonding with the family and praised the efforts of Competent Foundation.

YUGMARG NEWSPAPER —

Nadda, Hry CM, unveil 'Sunrays for Friday' book — "While speaking on the occasion, the Union Minister, J.P. Nadda shared that he enjoyed the 'Thought of the Day' message which was sent by Sanjay Tandon everyday along with his morning cup of tea. Appreciating the efforts of the couple for writing the series of books, the union minister said, "I have always felt that the ultimate happiness lies in the spirituality and the book 'Sunrays for Friday' along with other five encourages everyone to follow the path which takes us closer to the Higher truth."

He said that all the books written by the couple contained best of the stories which can be incorporated in our daily life. He especially praised Priya Tandon who has made beautiful sketches in the Sunrays Series. While sharing some notes on the book, Sanjay Tandon, who is also the founder of Competent Foundation, said, "It is an emotional day for me and I will always remain thankful to parents who have instilled spiritual values in me. Somehow my spiritual strength has inspired me to write inspirational stories in our books which are meaningful for the age group of 8 to 80 years. Now, I advise the younger generation to spend more time on inner-net than internet. I am sure our books will help people understand the deeper meaning of life." Earlier, five books in the 'Sunrays' series include Sunrays for Sunday, Sunrays for Monday, Sunrays for Tuesday, Sunrays for Wednesday and Sunrays for Thursday.

The first two books – Sunrays for Sunday and Sunrays for Monday have been published in Hindi and Telugu as well. And, what's more, the proceeds from the sale have gone for charity. The Sunrays series of books started out as a stand-alone book containing a collection of inspirational short stories titled 'Sunrays for Sunday'. The idea was to give food for thought to the readers to share a story with their children during family time, whether at the dining table or otherwise.